Lunatiques

by

S.N. Kirby

Lunatiques

Here there be Lunatiques, in this city settled on an island made of steel and bones. They roam through the mismatched buildings, passing in and out of time and place as if it were the most natural thing in the world. Lunatiques wander the streets with their blood so boiling hot they could slip their skins right off and keep on walking. Some may call them strange and insane, but I call them family, for they are the children of the moon.

I birthed them in the changing tides of the sea, pulling at their heartstrings and shaping them with the shifting glow of my moonbeams as their earth casts shadow between me and the sun. When the world and I were born, I watched from high above, content enough in doing just that. Everything changed when humans came into the world. They were—and still are— messy and complicated creatures, but there's beauty in all that heap of mess they make. Life on earth became more than just living. There were stories being told again and again, with endings twisting and turning in ways which both delighted and saddened me in that bittersweet quality called living.

The world is a deeply imperfect place, I see it all from above. Yet, there is so much wonder in it that I think I must be so big just to hold space for it all. I am moved by the simplest of things: a hand reaching out, a heartfelt confession, a secret embrace, or a vow made to live a truer self. The more I witnessed, the more I wished to shed my planetary skin for something more compact, so that I may too, slip in between the crowds on a hot day in June. I longed to feel smoke filled lungs breathing in the ash and heat of the city. I dreamt of being in the nose picking banality of the mundane.

Years of wishing and wanting without relief were such pain, but in that, something was created that I could have never expected. My tears poured out of me and magic rained down upon the earth. Down to earth this new magic fell and fulfilled the wish that I could never have. This is how the

1

impossible became possible. The sun may have brought life, but I brought magic.

Here is where a new kind of living was born in this world of man and magic. What came next were wonders I still don't understand. As I moved and changed in the reflection of the sun, so too did my Lunatiques change in the shifting light of my moonbeams. The transformation I so badly wished for myself, became possible for those born under the sign of the moon.

And so, I birthed you and others just the same, my little Lunatiques, to live as you dream and wish to be the thing you know you are. The world is full of darkness, but even as you look upon me you can see that there is light in the dark. I could tell you a thousand stories over and over that tell you the same. So, as you sleep and dream, I am here. When you reach out to me, I hold you in the way I can with all the magic and moonlight I possess.

Trash Moon Lives!

I am not a shiny thing. I live a single-serving kind of life, without a husband or a wife, and only my empty pockets to keep me company. Underneath my thread-bare suits, my body rots with each strange new pop and crack of my bones. I fear my usefulness is all used up and now I live on credit and borrowed time.

Such was my mood that still summer night, when the heat of the city pressed against me like the hungry breath of a panting beast. I had spent the last of my money on dinner and drinks at a dark-lit pub and needed a rest from the merciless beating of the day-to-day. Do you know the feeling when the last of what you had is all used up and there's nothing coming again for a while? (I knew it only too well.)

In my dismal mood of wanting, the sweet siren song of the river called to me and I answered. Nature is still a respite for the poor. Trees don't want your money. Grasses don't mind if the shoes you use to walk upon them have holes. Clouds don't care if you look a mess. This is the company I preferred that night.

As I made my way toward the riverbank, I walked alongside piles of garbage that turned sidewalks into trenches. Bags of black, grey, blue, and clear plastic were pressed against one another in undignified heaps. In that moment I saw the city for what it was: a hungry thing ready to devour at will and want. I felt as if I, too, had been used up and spit out like a forgotten husk of some discarded thing. My body was too old, my pockets too empty, and my mind too far gone.

I traveled past high rises with tall shaky ladders crawling up their brick-layered sides, past the broken sound of long forgotten operas playing from old men's radios, and past headstones rising from the hill against the twilight sky. I walked until the quiet hit and thick cement roads gave way to neatly trimmed pebble paths. Electric street lights became trees. Fire hydrants turned into wild bushes. Old fashioned gas lamps threw light for shadows to play on the ground.

3

In the cool wind-swept breath of the river and the sweet smell of grasses, I escaped the hunger of the city. The sun had only just fallen behind stone cliffs, and there was a hint of purple still drawn in the sky. I readied my pipe for a moment of blissful contemplation, my fingers sticky and brown with the sweet remains of that devil's weed. With a pop and a light, I was soon leaning back on my old familiar bench along the water. The smoke drifted as a moonless sky darkened the night.

There was the briefest of moments where my view changed, as if the scenery shifted like an old film catching and releasing in a projector. At the time, I doubted that it had even happened. Now I wonder if it wasn't some kind of key to understanding the night's events. I think it must have been a kind of slipping, as if by some energetic transportation I was brought into a world that looked very much like my own, but was not. As if by some unnatural wonder, I was given sight into another world that exists, physically at least, on our same plane, but cannot be accessed without a change of energy, be that by some wave or slip in the machine. After righting itself, the moment turned back into place.

I heard the jingling of loose coins before I saw him. Then, in a clearing where the path pokes out of the woods, I watched a shadow walking tall and loose. I don't usually pay attention to the strangers that roam through this little oasis of nature, but the way he sounded and the way he walked made me pause and stare. His body moved freely in his silhouette, and the corresponding clinks of coins made it seem as if his bones were as loose as the change in his pockets. I could see he was dressed in a suit with an expert cut that had been worn for several years too long. (I had one of those too.) He held himself with the air of an older gentlemen, yet possessed the sprightly body of a teenage boy. With a tilt of his head, he walked towards the bench next to mine.

From his coat pocket he pulled out a pipe and matches. His long fingers dragged the thin piece of match wood against the rough strike of the box. Smells of opium and jasmine sprung from the top of his newly-lit pipe. His stone-chipped teeth shined under the light of the lamp and gave his face an unholy glow. Smoke curled around his frame. He sat down and leaned back with a kind of supernatural satisfaction.

"Can't think of a better way to spend the morning," he said.

"You must be confused," I blurted. (I can't stand to leave an error uncorrected.) "The sun sets in the west." I motioned with my pipe. "It went behind the cliffs an hour ago."

"Evening?" He knocked his pipe against the metal arm of the bench.

"What have you been doing all day?" I asked.

"I don't know."

"You have no idea?"

"None whatsoever." His countenance was cool and calm as he shrugged.

"Could you have been asleep?" I wondered, aloud.

"Wouldn't I remember?" He replied.

"Suppose you didn't," I suggested.

"Suppose you're right and I have in fact, with no recollection, spent the day asleep somewhere and woke up just now from a sleep walk believing it was morning."

"Well now that that's cleared up, I suppose you feel much better."

"Yes, I do. Thank you very much!" He lifted a small stained bag from his coat pocket and filled his pipe once more. We sat in silence as clouds drifted against the dark sky.

"Do you think you might want to tell someone where you are?" I eventually asked.

"Why would I do that?" He looked startled.

"In case you missed something."

"What's today?"

"Wednesday."

"Wednesday!" He leapt from his seat. "I have to go!" Before he left, he turned towards me. "Would you like to go to a party?"

Now, it's important for you to know that I keep my schedule just the same every day. I awake in my dismal apartment with one sink, one toilet, and two small windows that overlook the dirty courtyard of the building next door. I make my coffee, read (scholarly journals, classic texts, newspapers, free pulp, women's magazines from the laundry room, etc.), and grade my undergraduates' papers on the uselessness of the out-of-print texts I teach. I leave for the university. I give my lecture. I come home by way of a pub for drinks, sometimes for dinner too, and I take my smoke—no exceptions.

However, that night I had the inclination to break away from the banality of my pathetic existence. Perhaps it was in the way he smelled, or the way he talked, or the smoke in his pipe that was the instrument for working his magic upon my mind, but I found him irresistible. I could have stayed and pouted for my empty pockets, but it wouldn't have changed their volume anyway.

"Lead the way," I replied, without a pause or a moment of doubt.

As we walked the path along the river, I noticed things that seemed at odds with my memory. For example, there are hidden areas where the shoreline juts down and gives way to beaches. Those parts belong to drifters who make shelters in rocks and caves. Without question, there is an unspoken rule between us and them: the unseen world is theirs. The casual passerby could see signs of them here and there; such as stumps and stones arranged in circles near the banks or ashes in the rocks they use as ovens to cook fish and eels from the river. Tonight, however, I saw nothing of them.

Instead, what I saw were the remnants of another sort of hidden people that gathered in the trees. They left behind sticks that extended out from branches that, I feared, were used for the roasting of pigeons. Discarded on the lower branches were crumbling hammocks made from young wood and vines. Clothes and shoes hung amongst the leaves to dry.

"What is this event?" I asked him as we continued along the path. "Some kind of fundraising thing?"

"You could say raising," he answered with a wicked look. "Funds, not so much."

6

"Around here?"

He gave a nod. "Just up the way, by the old graveyard."

"I know it," I said as I sunk my hand in my coat pocket, feeling the fabric as if it would ground me.

Unlike other graveyards you find pocketed in odd corners of the city, this one spanned across avenues with copper crypts of old and prestigious families forever clutching at rotting threads and tattered minks. I often felt as if those bodies and I decayed under the gravity of time and neither they nor I could stop the inexorable push towards deterioration. As we passed, I felt the breath of the grave pouring down upon my skull and I shuddered in my wrinkled skin.

The roads were quiet as we made our way back to the city streets. Something lighter than a fog had settled in between the maze of buildings. In the bright glow of the windows, I watched lights flicker on and off as figures moved in and out of rooms. On every street corner, old men smoked cigars with thick clouds of smoke dancing above their heads.

Curious, I thought. Where just earlier the same sidewalks had been buried under piles of garbage, they were now bare. The slickness of the streets seemed too clean, too scrubbed, as if someone had gone inch by inch and removed every last bit.

"We've almost just missed the beginning," he said as he picked up his pace.

"I didn't realize we had a schedule," I replied as I followed in suite.

"It's no good after they've started," He pulled out a thick cream-colored invitation from inside his pocket. "I'm sure you can only imagine how picky they are."

"I'm sorry, I can't." And I couldn't.

"Hah!" He said with a wink and a slap to my shoulder.

Now maybe the drinks I had at the pub earlier made me particularly open to the idea, but I surprised myself at how ready I was to let a stranger deliver me into the hands of some unknown fate. I felt as if some core component of ourselves

7

drew us together like magnets pulled apart for too long. He was intoxicating. The life around him vibrated so strongly that I felt as if I too were vibrant in his presence. I wanted to breathe him into me.

However, his face was unsettling. His features would shift. Just as I thought I would catch a glimpse of his countenance the pieces would scramble and blur. He had a sort of vaporous quality, as if what I was seeing was only a mist moving over a liquid body. It was like he was built differently than you and I.

The building ahead of us, normally dark and closed, was lit as if for a party. A carpet had been rolled out as a sort of greeting for guests, but there were none. No cars lined up to usher in women in long dresses or men in bright tuxes. Palm fronds and leaves lingered at windows like children watching from their nurseries. Hidden in the shadows of the door were two large men in dark suits standing sentry. My companion approached and with a wave of the invitation and a nod from the guards, we entered.

Crystal lamps spun webs of light on veined marble floors. Embossed furniture with fat velvet cushions lined the long hall. In an adjacent room, there was a large table laid out with piles of embonpoint fruits, rounds of cheese, cured meats, hot pies, roasted fowls, and towers of chocolate delights. My stomach ached! Never before had I seen such wealth laid out in front me!

"Party's this way," my companion said as he grabbed my elbow and steered me in the opposite direction.

"Are you sure?" I asked, still imagining the towers of champagne that surely awaited us in the rooms beyond. "Shouldn't we at least try the buffet to be polite?"

"Why would you want to mess with that garbage?" He said with an expression of disgust.

What kind of snobbish monster was this? Before I could tell him about the hard-working classes that furthered the mind and not the belly, about the good people that would not—could not—refuse such a feast no matter how trivial or gauche it might appear to the more fortunate parties, and about the right the human body has to being well fed, he opened a door. Down we went.

We made our descent along a spiraled staircase that began with the dimensions of a grown man, but slowly began to shrink in size until we were both cramped and crouched. Sounds of a party grew louder the deeper we went. At last, the space widened as we made our way to the landing at the foot of the stairs.

"They're not one for code around here, are they?" I said as I shook out the kinks that had settled in my body.

"Code?" He asked in a feigned attempt at interest.

At that moment, we had arrived at the top of a grand stone staircase. As I looked out towards the great hall, my legs shook and faltered beneath me in shock. Below us danced thousands upon thousands of crawfish shells, oyster halves, skeletons of fowl, and all matter of things that had been discarded from the restaurants and tables of the city. They danced in a kind of restrained fervor, as if they could not be contained by the formalities of steps in a waltz or a foxtrot. At first, the pieces appeared whole, but the closer I watched the more I noticed a missing leg here or a chipped shell there. That didn't seem to matter much to the dancers or their partners. They accommodated for the missing pieces deftly, in both form and decorum. At no point in the dance was any creature denied a partner for lack of a small claw or antenna.

An orchestra of spiders, beetles, and all manner of small bugs filled the chamber with music. If you have not heard the music of insects, then you have not experienced the sounds of angels. What lightness! What delicacy! Perched in corners of the cave, they strung their tiny wings and limbs against small webs in the crevices. With each pull across those misty strings, musical notes pulsed and vibrated to make melody and harmony.

Along the walls and ceiling, human bones had been pressed into intricate designs that depicted astrological constellations and celestial bodies. A bundle of heads interlaced to make a mosaic of a planet with teeth circled around to form rings. A line of femurs mapped out a constellation, with patella marking the placement of the stars. In the raucous mess of dancing bones, I wondered when I too would be placed in that chamber. Could my body be made into a replica of Saturn, or worse, Uranus?

"What a strange gathering," I remarked as we made our descent.

"I suppose it's as strange as any other." He gave me a sideways look and then shrugged. "When was the last time you went out?"

"I didn't think it was that long . . ."

"Come," he laughed and regained his genial composure. "Let's drink!"

We picked our way through the dance floor, careful not to crush our dancing counterparts. Once, or twice, I thought I saw the fist of a crawfish shaking angrily at me, but of course I could not be sure. We stopped at a gutter jutting from the wall. The spigot emerged from the open mouth of a ghoulish cherub and fed into a stone trough.

Animal carcasses and bones lounged along the sides upon rocks and coffins. Naturally, they were talking and joking with one another in a language I didn't know. If I had to guess, I would have said that it was a kind of Roman based language with Germanic sounds made up of clacking and smashing of teeth and bone for emphasis.

My contrapuntal party-goer returned with stone mugs of foul-smelling liquid. He handed one to me and said, "I take it this is your first full moon party?"

I sniffed at dregs that lingered on the mug's stone edge, gagging on fumes of what could only be putrid mushrooms and wood rot, but not before I could correct him.

"I'm sorry to say that I think you're mistaken again. It's a new moon tonight."

"Of course, it is!"

I stared at him, my face undoubtedly revealing my sin of ignorance.

"We're here," he said with a shake of his head, as if trying to explain something to a child or a very dumb man, he explained, "to make a new moon."

10

I think it must have been then that I started to wonder if perhaps I was in a world that was not my own. (You may think the dancing crawfish would have been the thing, but I assure you it felt very natural.) As I looked around at the bones and the shells around me, I realized that this must have been the equivalent of their galactic flotsam and jetsam, their collection of cosmic castoffs.

A gong rang from somewhere below us. The music stopped and the dancers halted their revelry. As if caught up in a kind of magnetic pulse, the little skeletons began to move towards an entrance to a dark and wide tunnel. With a nod from my new friend, I followed.

Light bulbs on strings lined either side of our path and illuminated the otherwise dark tunnel. Nothing extravagant had been added to make the place more comfortable or beautiful, which gave it an industrial feel that the miners had only left hours ago. We walked along a sloping path with large windows carved into the packed earth that offered views of the procession ahead, behind, and across the way. Curious skeletons hopped onto the window ledges to peer down at the thing below us.

We turned the corner and the mechanics of the operation were revealed. A propulsion chamber had been buried deep into the earth and gave the entirety of the space a long cylinder shape that dropped down from the surface. At the very top was a round brass covering with intricate pieces that interlocked at varying angles to give the door a mechanical mish-mash appearance. The walls of the chamber were smooth and made of polished brass.

Wheels and pulleys hung on thin copper wires, tucked in corners of the window outcroppings. Spindles extended like legs of crabs on ocean-wet rocks. Steam spouted out of chimney-like creations as parts churned and lifted in an endless cycling of constant movement. Everywhere, the place was alive with sounds of machine and bone.

Subtle vibrations on the floor alerted us to the great mechanical engine that whirled to life underneath. I peeked down to see the machine working in a series of pushing and

11

pulling to lift up, from somewhere even farther below us, a massive ball of planetary proportions that was set in the barrel of the chamber. Instead of the moon rocks one would expect, this body was made from the garbage of the city. Squished here and there were bits of paper, crinkled plastic package, stained cardboard, disintegrated garbage bags, half-eaten food, faded clothing, crushed bottles, and ripped magazines.

"It's time!" My companion exclaimed. "It's been so long since I've been up!"

"Up?" I shook my head. "I'm afraid I'm still unfamiliar with the logistics."

"When they raise the moon, I'm going up with it," he said with a smile. "I don't suppose you'd like to do the same?"

We walked farther and farther down with sounds of small things clicking and clacking resounding around the packed earth.

"Up." I whispered.

"Yes, up."

"Wouldn't you be missed?" I asked.

"Oh," he waved his hand as if swatting a bug, "I always make it down with the rest."

"The rest?"

"Well yes, how do you expect it all to stay up there?"

Illumination took hold of my mind and I asked, "You mean to tell me, that the phases of the moon are the subtle falling apart of its body?" I imagined it falling, piece by piece, back down to the earth and into the oceans and mountains of the landscape.

"Well yes, if you're looking for an elementary explanation," he said offhandedly.

As the moon made of trash was raised higher, bones and skeletons began to hop onto the body and cling to its sides as they created a city, a people, of forgotten and discarded things. Some of them continued the revelry from the ballroom and grabbed partners to dance. Others began burrowing into the sides and rearranging the bits of garbage, as if setting up camp. Still, some began climbing down the sides and swinging from the bits of trash that poked up past the surface. Everywhere there was a sense of immense anticipation.

"I like to go up when I feel lackluster or beat down and broken," my companion said as he watched waves of little skeletal bodies jumping and plunging onto the colossus of the new moon. Together they were beginning to form mountains and crevices. "I find it happens most often when I've just been dragged down again by cruel gravity."

"I see my return as an act of defiance.," he continued as he lifted his hands upwards and motioned towards the sky. "I take offense that an invisible force should decide where I belong." He lifted the skeleton of a bird. "And so, I return again and again," he said. The bird wiggled in a playful way beneath his grasp. The bones of its wings fluttered with excitement. He gave the spine a long stroke. "Not to mention that these wonderful creatures are such fun."

What I had mistaken for a strange man with a strange invitation, I now recognized to be the grand maestro of it all. The two of us stood alone on the hard earth of the tunnel.

"Shall we?" He asked as he turned to me once more.

This alchemical transformation he offered seemed too surreal. How could it be that these broken things were made glorious with the ghostly light of the sun? Of course, what is a moon if not the impersonal crashing and chaos of the universe coming together to make something beautiful out of the detritus. When we contemplate these celestial bodies, we forget that they were not made that way. No, they too were once the discarded. If such things could be made into the greatness, then perhaps I too, could also have such hopes for redemption.

I gave a nod and with my old frail body I added myself to that batch of waste. We landed with a soft thud on a bed of papers and fabric. Above us, the brass door pulled back to reveal open sky. Sounds of clicks and locks filled the room as a spring pulled back and drew our moon deeper into the earth until it could go no farther.

Like a pebble in a slingshot, the moon lurched forward with a release of energy and motion. We rattled through the

13

barrel with such force that I almost could not breathe. The sky drew closer as we moved towards the top of the barrel. With the sound of an explosion, we were sprung up into the sky! Flames flickered behind us as I watched us move into the air. Below us the river twinkled with the reflections of our fire. All the while the little crustaceans waved goodbye.

As if the worker of the machine recognized his mistake and righted me again, my next memory was of sitting alone on my bench along the river. I felt at the bits of crawfish shell that littered my pants, to remind myself that it had been real, that I had been there. A loneliness came upon me as I thought of them up in the sky, while I was left here below on earth.

Still, I am here on this bench, waiting again for the day I return once more. Until then, I will tell my story to all who will listen. For there is a world in our strange universe that finds beauty and grace in the broken and discarded. As surely as I am alive and here with you, I tell you, trash moon lives!

Emmaline and the Beautiful Wendigo

Saturday in Central Park was always a zoo, but with the unusually warm November air dancing around the bright gold and blood red leaves in the soft light of the setting sun, the park was practically a riot. Music played all around Emmaline. The trumpet from the jazz band up the hill heralded the sunset in high notes while an oscillating beat popped in swift rhythms from the drum circle in a small thicket of trees. A slow tango from another time and place drifted through the din as women in low heels and men in loose suits dipped in that slow way, looking like phantoms among the living.

From her perch on top of the rock, Emmaline could coolly survey it all. No matter what interesting thing was happening below she could not pull her eyes away from the tops of the tall buildings around her. They were mysterious realms far above with balconies impossibly high up in the air and large windows in strange shapes that hinted at large and mysterious rooms behind them. Emmaline ignored the crowds swarming below her as she rested against the cool gray stone with her head tilted up toward the sun. When she looked up at the upper floors of these grand buildings from so far below, she thought that these must be the homes of the gods for they seemed worlds away from her and just as full of unknowable mysteries. She supposed their inhabitants could be inhuman, if not even fully divine.

When at last the warmth of the sun gave way to a chill that was not yet biting, but perhaps nibbling, Emmaline gathered herself and joined the crowds streaming out of the park to go to the next (warm) pleasant event they had lined up for the evening. Emmaline had no such plans. Only rarely did she ever have plans and it was always on someone else's dime. She suffered from the classic syndrome of having taste and class, but no money of her own. However, through a series of happenstance and circumstantial kinship, she found herself around wealth but always circumvented just outside of it. What she had gained from these associations was the luxury of laziness, which she had cultivated into an art.

Emmaline lounged about the sprawling pools of her wealthy acquaintances and drank Manhattan cocktails as a guest in private clubs all over the city. As she lounged and drank, Emmaline dreamt of treasures still unknown to her. Visions of grand estates with endless rooms and long winding corridors filled her head. Emmaline repeated over and over that she did not want to possess these treasures—too much work, she would say with a shake of her head—simply being around them was treasure enough for her. Although, she knew that wasn't true.

A pale blue dusk rolled across the city and the streetlights responded with their soft artificial glow that looked like stars captured from heaven. Pumpkins and squashes decorated the porches and steps of the lush Upper East Side neighborhoods. With a quick open of a small iron gate, Emmaline trotted down a hidden set of stairs below a grand stone townhome. She turned the key to the small door that led to her tidy room on the basement level of the house.

The house belonged to the family of a friend from college, Claire, whom Emmaline had befriended when a scholarship at an expensive school with a plethora of nearby thrift stores filled with designer castoffs made Emmaline seem more well off than she was. At graduation, Claire casually invited Emmaline to come stay with her family in the city, probably never expecting Emmaline to stay for longer than a weekend. She had been there nearly a year.

"Emmaline," a voice called out from above, "come upstairs! The flowers just arrived and they're divine!"

Emmaline rushed into the bathroom for a quick touch up and a spritz from a designer perfume sample. She needed to make sure she looked properly polished and coiffed. With a final ruffle and fluff of her clothes, she ascended the stairs into the main house.

Where the guest rooms in the basement level were maintained with the care of a hotel suite, the main house was maintained with the care and dedication of the Metropolitan

16

Museum of Art. Every piece of furniture and each little knick-knack was curated to convey an exact narrative of life in this house: one of travel, taste, and—above all—wealth.

Emmaline's steps echoed as she walked into the grand tone foyer with a rich cream marble floor. At its center was an older woman admiring a fresh orchid upon a vintage gold table. She touched the stem as if cordially welcoming a guest into her home for a brunch or holiday party.

"Grace, it's absolutely gorgeous," Emmaline gushed.

"Isn't it?" Grace said with a smile over her shoulder as Emmaline approached. "It's a, oh what does he call it again? I keep forgetting," she said with a shrug and a lift of her martini glass, "These certainly don't help with that." She swooped her arm through Emmaline's as they walked through the house.

"They remind me of the flowers we used for a party my dearly departed James and I threw back when we still owned that old apartment downtown." She leaned in closer, "I wish you could have seen me then! Oh, the guests we had! Now let me see, there were members of some royal family from the strangest little countries, musicians and opera singers, and wealthy businessmen from all over the world— half of whom I don't remember. How they all danced with the band and drank champagne, and we all felt like we were so young and still so full of dreams." She lifted her glass and took a long drink. "I shined that night!"

"I love your stories," Emmaline said as they walked into the parlor. A fire was roaring and a small spread of nibbles and an assortment of drinks and glasses had been served for the family's long-established ritual of a cocktail hour, which was still insisted upon by Grace. Emmaline helped herself to a glass of wine and a cracker topped with an artichoke spread.

"You're my favorite audience, darling, and really, I mean that wholeheartedly," Grace said as she finished her martini and helped herself to another from the shaker. With a wink, she popped an olive in her mouth.

"Just us tonight?" Emmaline asked.

Emmaline adored Grace, who was exactly the kind of woman she wished had been her mother. Her own mother was a disappointment who constantly embarrassed Emmaline with her clothes from big box discount stores, two-in-one shampoo and conditioner, and spreads of butter crackers with canned cheese. She was drab and ordinary. More horrifying to Emmaline was that she was perfectly happy being that way.

"Oh, who knows," Grace said with a shrug and a sigh.

"Enough with the dramatics, Mother," said Claire as she walked into the room with bags from Bergdorf's and Sack's. "I'm here," she said as she kissed Grace's cheek.

"What's all that?" Grace asked as she poked her fingers into the bags and tore at the delicate tissue paper around the purchases.

"Clothes for a party tomorrow," she said as swopped the bags away from her mom and set them beside a loveseat. In one motion, she helped herself to a heavy pour from a bottle of vodka and mixed it with soda and a twist of lime.

"What party?" demanded Grace. "I don't know of anyone throwing any sort of social functions this week."

"That's because you don't know anyone anymore, Mother," Claire said as she kicked off her shoes, leaned back in the loveseat, and tucked her feet under her long legs.

Emmaline sat up straighter in the wing backed chair, giving her skirt a tug. She supposed that she would never be permitted to act so casually, but when she looked up from her skirt to see Claire watching her with curiosity and a hint of what she supposed was frustration, Emmaline couldn't understand why. Pretending as if the whole exchange hadn't happened, Claire dipped her hand into the bag and pulled out a dress that was so shiny and delicate it looked as if it had been spun from gold.

"Look," she said as she held it up to show Grace, "doesn't this remind you of what the dancers were wearing that night in St. Petersburg?"

"Oh!" Grace exclaimed as she leaned over to press her fingertips against the fabric, "It's wonderful, Claire. Is that what you're going to wear?"

"This," she said returning the dress to the bag, "or this crushed velvet dress." She teased open the bag to show the fabric to her mother, who had already returned to her martini.

"Whose party are you attending?" Emmaline asked, running through her own list of social events going on that month.

"An old money Dutch trader," Claire replied with a shrug, "That's what they tell me anyway."

"You should go together!" Grace declared as she turned to Emmaline.

"Why is that?" Asked Claire with a quick glance into her empty glass.

"Because I don't know who this person is and I don't trust you to give me an accurate report of the details." She took another sip of her martini. "I have to be in the know!"

"Sure," said Claire with a shrug, "you should come Emma."

"I'll give you one of my old dresses to wear," Grace said.

"I would love that," Emmaline said with a smile.

"Don't bother with those old drabby things." Claire said as she slid off the loveseat and helped herself to another vodka soda with lime. "You can wear one of mine," She gave Emmaline a look up and down, "If you're coming with me, I want you to look nice."

"My dresses are nice!" Grace scoffed.

"Nice, but old, Mother," Claire said as she bent down to give her a kiss on the cheek. "Don't be upset," she said, "I didn't mean anything by it."

"Fine," Grace agreed with a lift of her empty martini glass, "for the sake of the pleasantries of the evening" she said as she rose to get another drink.

"I promise not to say another word," said Claire. Under her breath she muttered to Emmaline, "at least not to her face."

Emmaline laughed offhandedly. This was exactly the kind of closeness they had shared in the early days of their friendship. Now, Emmaline felt that she was here as Grace's guest not Claire's. Her loyalties had shifted and the mockery felt like a betrayal, but not laughing along felt like one too. She knew Grace was lonely and thought that Claire was indifferent to her mother's loneliness. Spending time unwrapping old jewelry, drinking martinis at midday, and taking walks around the house to linger at artwork and antiques let Grace feel like Emmaline was a companion, but a companion that was more like a doll being played with by a young girl rather than an adult friendship. Emmaline didn't mind, however, because she was lonely too.

***

Late into the night, an unexpected deep freeze swept through the city. Water turned to ice on sight and brutal cold winds whipped through the avenues. A halo formed around the moon as the air itself turned to ice. Before the blizzard, the world stood frozen still.

Emmaline awoke to the sounds of radiators banging and hissing as they fought off the unexpected cold front. She walked to the basement window, looking up in disbelief. Snow fell in such thick droves that even the persistent glare of the streetlamps could no longer be seen.

Steam piped out of the tops of buildings like tea kettles on the stove. Their billows formed ominous shadows like monsters racing across the tops of buildings. The vision of their moving bodies loomed large overhead.

She watched as a snowflake moved toward her with such force and with such a straight trajectory that she could have sworn it was coming straight for her. At the last minute it dodged her with a quick turn. How silly, she thought, to believe that a single snowflake could have a will of its own and that it would single her out. She shook her head at the thought. These were nothing more than the wine drenched dreams of a scared little girl, she chided to herself.

With a smart snap of the curtains, Emmaline shut out the night and its horrid sounds of the winter storm. She turned the nozzle of the radiator to the left as far as it would go. With a shiver, she slid back into the soft down of the guest bed and snuggled under the thick comforter. The sudden comfort of the bed made her giddy and for a minute she did feel like a child once again. Only this time, she thought, she was finally where she belonged.

***

A sharp scream burst through the snowy silence of the morning. Emmaline lifted her head out from under the cozy den of down she had burrowed under in the night. With a stretch and a slither, she went to the window to see if it had all been a dream. When she pulled back the curtain, all she saw was snow piled high from the bottom of the barred pane to the top.

Halfway through her shower, Emmaline wondered what the scream had been all about anyway. As she dried her hair with the roaring of the hair dryer in her ear, she thought it must have been a reaction to the snow. Finally, with the last brush of blush on her cheek and flourish of her skirt, she concluded that it must have been a scream of surprise at the unexpected blizzard.

"You're here!" Claire exclaimed as she saw Emmaline and hugged her a little too tightly.

"Claire?" Emmaline said as she reeled backward and peeled Claire off her in confusion. She noticed the small voice coming from the phone ("Ma'am? Are you still there?") and tears streaming down her face.

"I'm here," Claire said as she gathered herself from Emmaline's rebuff and turned away from her. "Yes, she's upstairs. No," she continued, "she's not breathing."

Emmaline walked to the window, stunned and still. She watched the snowflakes continue to fall onto the blanketed city of white. Faintly, in the background, she could hear Claire talking to someone who must have known what to do or at least what to say. Emmaline knew the truth before she knew she did. No one could come for Grace in this weather.

"No one's coming," Claire said before covering her mouth and silently screaming into her hand. She steadied herself against an antique chair that Grace let absolutely no one sit in ever. Claire sat there, shaking.

"I have to see her," Emmaline said. She felt cold and numb.

"Please don't go," Claire said in between sobs, "Don't leave me."

"Wait here," Emmaline reassured her.

In response Claire curled up onto the floor, hiding her face in her knees and sobbing viciously and violently. Emmaline steadied herself against the banister and ascended the stairs alone for the first time. Rules hadn't been explicitly set, but never before had Emmaline ascended to the upper floors without the company of Grace or Claire. This was not a part of the house she was allowed to be in by herself and she couldn't help but feel giddy about it. She took her time arriving at Grace's bedroom.

The staircase spiraled upwards like the curling of a seashell, and Emmaline ran her hand along the railing as if it were her own. There was a shift happening within her that felt dangerous and reckless. She dipped into the rooms on the upper floors with leisure and a lack of concern for anything but the adoration of the things held in each of them. Emmaline picked up objects, admiring them intently as if they had been created for her pleasure alone. People responded differently to grief, Emmaline thought as she tried to rationalize her strange behavior. She had meant to go right to Grace's room, but somehow, she had ended up in the little pocket library on the fourth floor.

This went on, with her dipping and ducking into rooms far away from the one she meant to enter. She couldn't understand what was happening to her. She felt ashamed, but unable to stop. By the time she made it to Grace's room, Emmaline had explored every other room in the upper floors of the house.

Emmaline knocked on the door when she entered, even though she knew there wouldn't be a response on the other

22

side. In the darkness of the bedroom, Emmaline saw Grace lying in her bed uncovered. A martini sat on her bedstand where one might find a glass of water. Upon her death, Grace had soiled the bed, which added yet another horror. Emmaline went to the windows, pulled back the curtains, and opened them wide. A fresh gust of cold air blew into the stale room. The world was drenched in white, casting an artificial purity upon the otherwise dirtied and dark city. She watched the empty streets with wonder. Curious faces popped in and out of view from the neighboring windows, and peered out to marvel at the snow.

When Emmaline turned back from the window, she was shocked at the disarray of the room. Clothes and shoes were thrown wildly across the floor. An alarming amount of empty airplane liquor bottles and their separated tops were tossed across surfaces. Open makeup and lipstick containers littered the tops of dressers and vanities. She shook her head. The room certainly could not have been like this yesterday. She knew Grace drank, but this was something she had never seen. Of course, Emmaline thought as she pulled up a chair next to Grace's body, Grace employed several people to help her keep the house in order, prepare food, and otherwise attend to the things she did not want to attend to herself. Were it not for the blizzard, someone would have been here by now, hiding the truth from everyone, and perhaps even hiding it from Grace, herself.

Emmaline looked at the old woman before her. Lipstick and mascara smeared across her face and her bedclothes were only half on and misbuttoned. In that instant, the heroism of Grace diminished and Emmaline wondered what kind of life Claire really had under her mother's rule. Emmaline sat for a long time, shivering in the cold that came in through the open windows.

In a last testament to the afternoons that they had spent together, and the contrived tenderness they shared, Emmaline gathered the trash and clothes from the floor. She capped the lipstick and closed the compacts. With the care and attention of an undertaker, she wiped the smeared makeup from Grace's face and rebuttoned her pajamas. Emmaline pulled the sheet over her face and left the room.

She found Claire in the study clutching an opened bottle of scotch. The remnants of the previous evening's cocktail hour were still there. Only now, the fire was out and the neatly arranged snacks and drinks were scattered and spoiling. Emmaline began to clean under Claire's glare.

"You don't have to do that you know," Claire said practically spitting out the words.

"It shouldn't stay out here like this," Emmaline said.

"Now that mother's dead, I suppose you'll be leaving soon," she said. "Unless you're already auditioning for the role of the maid." She took another swig.

"I'm not," Emmaline managed to get out, still in shock. The truth was, she hadn't thought about the termination of her stay in the grand house.

"Don't forget your place around here," Claire said with another large gulp and gag. "You can't possibly imagine I would let mother's *plaything* stay in my house."

"Your house?" Emmaline repeated.

"What?" Claire said wickedly, "You thought it was yours now? Thought she might leave it to you?" She took another large gulp and in response threw up all over the floor. "I never could drink like her." She said in between heaving and retching.

Emmaline went to the kitchen for a glass of water. Her head was spinning as she began to understand the reality of her situation. The hand she held wasn't good and she wondered if she had ever played the game right at all. Here she was—after all those martinis and languid afternoons—about to be homeless when she had found a place that felt like home. She returned to the study with a full glass and fresh towels.

"Here," she said as she gave the water to Claire.

"We took you in," Claire said ignoring the water and taking a long drag from the bottle.

"Am I stray dog?" Emmaline asked as she took a bottle of club soda from the cocktail cart and poured it over the carpet. The melted ice from the ice bucket cleaned up the rest and provided a convenient place for Claire to vomit once more.

"A stray dog would have loved me more than you," Claire said as she lifted her head out of the bucket.

"Claire?" Emmaline asked with a quizzical look, "What do you mean?"

"I mean that she was my mother," Claire said rising from the ground, "I was the one who had to bandage her up when she fell down drunk," her voice grew louder, "I was the one who dragged her up the stairs when she was too pissed to even walk up the steps." She began to approach Emmaline, "I was the one she screamed at when she was blackout drunk in a blind rage!"

Emmaline could smell the scotch and vomit on Claire's breath. She had gotten so close to her that Emmaline couldn't tell if Claire was going to hit her or kiss her. Her pulse quickened and something inside her heart popped a little.

"She was my mother," Claire said as if remembering herself.

"That wasn't right, what she did," Emmaline said with a shake of her head, "I'm sorry, I didn't know."

"No one did." Claire responded, defeated by her own rage. "That was the point." She left the room still holding onto the bottle.

Emmaline busied herself, trying to not think about what had transpired between the two of them. There were so many secrets in the house. In the purity of the snowy morning, she was only beginning to understand the dirt that had been hidden right before her eyes. She felt foolish for being so blinded by the glitter of it all.

After she had finished tidying up the mess in the study, she began to find other ways to be helpful and occupy herself until the city shoveled itself out of the snow. Claire had locked herself in her room. Every now and then, Emmaline knocked and left water, soft drinks, juices, toast, cookies, soup and crackers, medicines to calm the stomach, little pills to help with headaches, and a wide variety of the herbal tinctures and tonics Grace had kept as remedies for her hangovers and "nerves." While Claire still refused to open the door, the little gifts were gone by the time Emmaline arrived to leave another helpful item.

When at last the paramedics arrived, the house was back to its clean and tidy self, and so was Claire. She showed them to her mother's room, while Emmaline hid out downstairs in the basement. The heat of the house had melted the snow just enough so that Emmaline could peek out on her tiptoes and watch the feet of the emergency medical technicians treading through the drifts of snow. After they left, Emmaline crept back upstairs. Claire was waiting for her.

"There you are," she said with a snap.

"Did they say what . . ." Emmaline drifted off and looked down at her feet, unwilling to say it out loud.

"What killed her?" Claire said with a touch of cruelty. "She died of a stroke after decades of drinking like the bottle would never run dry." She looked at Emmaline. "Funny how it's the things you love most that kill you in the end." Claire turned on her heels and marched upstairs, but not before throwing Emmaline an agitated look over her shoulder. "Well, come on now. We have to get ready."

"For what?" Emmaline asked.

"For this party," Claire replied as if it were the most obvious thing in the world.

"Now?" Emmaline said still in stock. "After what's happened?"

"I can't stay here anymore," Claire shuddered unconsciously before regaining her composure. "Come on," she said with a wave, "I want to see how it looks."

"How what looks?" Emmaline inquired following Claire upstairs.

"The dress I picked out for you," she said as she opened the door to her room.

"You picked out a dress for me?" Emmaline couldn't understand what was happening.

26

"Not like you could afford your own," she said as she gave Emmaline a look. "You didn't think you fooled anyone with those consignment clothes you wore in college, did you? Half of them were from my closet. How could I not recognize them?"

Emmaline almost cried. She leaned in the doorway, clutching her stomach. So much of her world was crumbling so quickly that she barely trusted the floor to be there beneath her. For so long, she had constructed her entire life to hide who she was entirely. She believed that if people knew, they would shun her as she did to her own mother. Then again, she thought, Claire did know and befriended her anyway.

"Come," Claire softened when she saw Emmaline's reaction. She touched her arm and gently pulled her into the room.

Emmaline breathed in the dusky fragrance Claire wore in lieu of the flowery and fresh smells most of her contemporaries spritzed onto themselves by the bucket load. She had always liked how different Claire was from everyone else. When they were in college, the two of them would spend long afternoons after classes laying on the floor of Claire's dorm room listening to the vintage records she collected.

They had found the old record player at a nearby flea market on a rainy afternoon and Claire became obsessed. She collected any kind of record she could get her hands on, which included everyone from Duke Ellington and John Coltrane to Carl Carlton. They would lay there listening to old records over and over, scarfing down chocolates and candies, which Grace had banned from the house when Claire was still a small child. High on sugar and the sounds of Billie Holiday, they would laugh and lay there until dusk fell, and they would at last be brought back to reality with the stomping of stilettos marching down the hall to pull Claire out of her sugar coma to expensive dinners and nearby nightclubs, which Emmaline could never afford.

***

The snow stopped, and Claire was drunk before they even got into the car. Emmaline now understood the stress she must have felt at having to manage Grace in these states, which was a delicate balance of watching and pretending not to watch all at once. She popped open her compact mirror and reapplied her dark red lipstick, all the while eying Claire from the side. Ice clinked in the cocktail Claire had brought with her into the car. She let the liquid swish around haphazardly as she leaned her head against the glass and looked out the window.

Claire looked like a thousand stars in her gold dress that lingered just past her knees. Her hair pooled around her face in loose curls that shined in the light of the passing streetlamps. Emmaline shifted in the full length, red, crushed velvet dress with sleeves that fell around her shoulders and a decolletage that dipped low enough to be revealing, but not too low as to be inappropriate. She topped off the dress with full length gloves she borrowed from Grace's closet. Her dark lipstick and manicured hair made her look like a Doris Day dream. Both girls wore Grace's diamonds as a kind of homage to the recently departed. Only when they entered the car did Emmaline wonder why she was still letting someone else play dress her up like a doll.

"We're here," Emmaline said with a light touch on Claire's knee.

"Already?" Claire asked lazily, barely bothering to move. With a look at Emmaline's hand, she rolled down the window and tossed out the rest of the drink. She took the hand still on her knee and let Emmaline guide her out of the car. The heel of her gold boots tripped on the ice of the curb, and she flailed about wildly before catching her balance then pretending as if the whole incident hadn't happened.

"Up we go," she said as she shook off Emmaline and her faux fur coat.

Someone had cleared a path in the sidewalk from the street to the building's entrance. Emmaline breathed a sigh of relief. Neither of their heels were made for ice or snow, but she was more worried that Claire would fall hard and fast against the concrete. Cars were lining up behind them to enter. This was quite the party, Emmaline thought as she watched the other guests arrive and linger at the elevator.

"Darling," a young woman with impossibly long blonde hair, a tight black dress, and sky-high stilettos gushed as she ran to embrace Claire, "you look divine."

"Would you expect anything less?" Claire asked a little too smugly, probably a biproduct of the amount of booze pumping through her system.

With that, Emmaline disappeared from the conversation, and Claire transformed into the pompous prep school brat she so desperately tried to escape. A gaggle of perfectly polished young women pulled her into their circle, catching the elevator and closing the door on Emmaline. Emmaline cursed herself for even coming to the event. She tapped her shoes uncomfortably as those left in the lobby eyed her suspiciously, or even with pity at the social snafu she had endured. With a noncommittal smile, Emmaline set herself to look pleasant and unbothered. Of course, she was bothered, and vowed not to talk to a single person the entirety of the party. She so desperately wished that she and Claire were spending the evening in their pajamas watching old movies and eating a dinner of cookies and candies from the bodega down the street.

When the elevator returned to the world below, Emmaline slipped into the back, unseen and barely noticed. Everyone else was doing a well enough job pretending she wasn't there, which was just fine by her. If she could pose just the right way in key moments, she could get away with barely being noticed. Really, she was only staying because she was worried about Claire. This was the most time the two of them had spent together since their days in college and Emmaline was beginning to wonder how she had let so much space and time pass between them. They were close, once.

Emmaline heard the music before they reached their destination. Only after she saw the light of the elevator button disappear, did she realize they arrived at the top of one of the many buildings she had daydreamed about just yesterday. The doors opened to a grand and full hall with waiters carrying trays with passed canapes, dancers reveling to the music of an old-fashioned swing band, and cold drinks sweating and clinking with the conversations that bubbled up between sips.

She picked up a glass of champagne from a passing tray, and made her way around the party. Keeping to the edges of the crowd, Emmaline passed in and out of the rooms that never seemed to end. At last, she found a gorgeous pair of full-length doors that opened up to the outdoor patio. A sharp gust of cold wind blew in as she went outside.

A full winter garden draped in a crisp white blanket of snow greeted her. Paths had been cleared between the plants. The trees reached upwards with their icy branches in supplication of the bright moon above them. Couples braved the cold for clandestine kisses and cigarettes, although they, and Emmaline, knew the host would probably not approve of either.

She walked through the paths, marveling at the grandness of the building and the extensive gardens the snow hid. How was all this even possible she wondered? The apartment itself was not an apartment at all, but rather a mansion plopped on top of a building complete with large white columns, and even separate guest houses and a pool, which the freezing temperatures turned into an ice rink.

Everything about the house and the party itself felt so out of time and place. There was an oldness disguised as classic that made Emmaline wonder about the party and the host, who she still had not met. There were some people she recognized in passing, but no one she knew. Emmaline noted how little congeniality there was between the guests, outside of those who arrived together. The guest list seemed like a random culling of the mailing lists for the high society social clubs of the city with little regard for who actually attended. No one knew each other here, not really, but they were all connected by a singular thread: wealth, or at least the appearance of it.

Emmaline slipped back inside to the noise and chaos of the party. Claire must have received an invitation from the girls she had run into downstairs, Emmaline thought as she reached for a passing canape and another champagne. She passed a decadent dining room with a full spread of fruits, nuts, cheeses, breads, and piping hot silver dishes filled with such delicious smelling things that made her head spin and stomach growl. A line around the table formed as guests piled food on top of plates, and waiters refilled the emptying containers with punctilious dedication.

Discarded porcelain plates and silverware were scooped up the moment they were placed down with such alacrity that one might wonder if they were there at all. In an adjacent room, the same act played out with a large table full of cakes, pastries, macaroons, chocolate covered fruits, and about a thousand other sweets that Emmaline had never seen before, but looked so delectable that she felt compelled to try them all. She was just about to pick up a particularly scrumptious looking dark chocolate mousse when she saw Claire pass by the doorway.

Her heart froze a beat when she saw her. Something did not seem right. She abandoned the dessert table to follow Claire from a distance like a guardian angel, unseen and watching. Claire was still with the group of girls from the elevator with their long hair, high heels, and manicured hands that dipped into their small purses for pills to fit the mood. Claire looked reckless and wild. She was teetering on her heels and holding onto the walls. One of the girls gave her a look and with a whisper to another they sat her down and left her all alone.

Claire's head bobbed as she slumped deeper into the chair. Her wild curls fell around her face in a golden cloud. Emmaline scooped her up in one quick motion and took her to one of the endless rooms. Most were occupied by one elicit act or another, but an empty summer dining room with hard stone floors and tall columns sufficed.

In the summer, the room would have been wonderful with the glass doors open to the warm breeze. The patio overlooked the dotted lights of the city and the life below pulsing and pumping like the blood of a wild thing. In the ice crusted night, the room was freezing. No doubt that unbearable cold in addition to the brutal severity of the furniture (a thick and heavy table lined with high backed and desperately uncomfortable looking chairs) made this room decidedly empty and neglected.

"Did you take anything?" Emmaline asked as she sat Claire down at the table.

"Like . . . silverware?" Claire responded as she laid her head on the table.

"If silverware gets you this trashed." Emmaline said, sounding more annoyed than she meant.

"So now you're the funny one?" Claire said, lifting her head off the table.

"I'm not trying to be funny, Claire," Emmaline said. "I'm trying to help you. Please, let's go home."

"It's not *your* home," Claire said. "It's my home and I'll go when *I* say, not *you*."

"This isn't you," Emmaline pleaded.

"Isn't it?" Claire stood and wobbled on her heels, "It was who my mother was. Why shouldn't it be me?"

"Because you're different," Emmaline said trying to coax her to sit down. "You saw me for who I was, when I was trying so hard to hide it from everyone, including myself. Please, Claire, let's call it a night."

"I saw you," Claire said as she swayed. "and I *loved* you—can you believe it!? Loved you . . . and what?" She tossed her hands wildly in the air, nearly losing balance. "You left me to play pretend with *her.*" She nearly keeled over herself. "And now you—what? Want to act like it didn't happen? Like you didn't pull away from you every time I needed you?" Claire went straight up to Emmaline and pressed her body against hers. "You weren't there." She said with her face so close to Emmaline's they shared the same breath. Tears fell down her cheeks.

"Whatever," Claire said. She brushed off her tears and staggered out of the room.

"Wait," Emmaline called out after Claire. The thought of Claire's closeness to her created the same heart thumps she had felt earlier in the study. There was a madness to the feeling she couldn't control any longer. "Claire," she said as she rushed after her and grabbed her arm.

"No!" Claire ripped her arm away from Emmaline. She spun away and tripped over her heels. then fell and hit her head on the table before bouncing onto the cold stone floor. She shivered and then stopped. Blood pooled all around her.

Emmaline dropped to the floor beside her, shaking uncontrollably. Any warmth left in her body went out in a single breath. Her heart felt as if it had stopped beating in her chest and her vision was growing darker by the second.

"Well," a voice said from above, "I didn't expect this." A man with sharp features stepped into the room and closed the door behind him. Emmaline thought that with his expensive tuxedo and broad shoulders, he could have walked straight out of an advertisement in Time Square.

"She . . ." Emmaline tried to talk, "she just," her voice caught in her breath and she was unable to say any more.

"I know what happened," the handsome stranger said coolly as he stepped over the body. He sat down at the table as if Claire's dead body were the most natural thing in the world.

"You killed her," he said.

"I-I-I," stuttered Emmaline "didn't!"

"Save your words," he replied, "because you and I both know that's not how anyone's going to see it." He motioned for her to sit at the table, "Please, sit."

"I can't—"

"SIT!" He yelled.

Emmaline pulled at the nearest chair and sat down at the table. His words stung, but her desire for the rhythm of authority and obedience compelled her to sit.

"Now," he said, "I know everyone who walks into my home. I know who's important and who's not." He leaned in towards her, "Let me tell you that you're not."

She lowered her eyes in silence.

"Good," he said, "I like that you're not going to fight me on that one. It shows a strength of character to know where you truly stand in the world."

Emmaline sat still, but she could feel her heart beating wildly. Her body felt the fear there first, only now had it begun to take over her mind. She knew this man would kill her.

"Now, let me tell you who I am." He leaned back in his chair. "My story is true, this much at least. I am a Dutch trader. Although, what I don't tell others is that I came to this island before it was anything like the city it is today."

"My indiscretions," he said, "cast me out of my home and to this New World, where I could walk amongst others running from their past toward a brighter, if not newer, future than they could have had. When I saw this place, I didn't see it for what it was, but what it could be...No, would be. I felt as if the hand of God came down from the sky to show me this great city so I could take it for my own."

"I had the sight and vision, but no means by which to achieve this grand purpose. More and more colonists came to this land each day, with their own means and resources, taking more and more away from what should be mine."

"When everything I had ran dry, I was once again cast out into the wilderness. I went past the wall the Dutch had built and forged along the Hudson River. I was hungry and desperate, barely surviving another day in the brutal and cold winter. While I roamed, I came upon a man with a home and a family who had not known hunger like I had. I began to stalk him like an animal. For days, I returned to watch him and his family with their warm furs and endless food. One day, I stole his axe."

Emmaline let the corner of her eyes rest on Claire, who laid on the floor beside her. Her body looked so still on the cold floor. Emmaline so desperately wished they had not come. She wished everything had turned out differently.

"I waited until night fell," the mand continued, " and I slaughtered him and his family, just to feast upon what he had." His lips curled around his teeth. "But I wasn't the only one hunting that day."

"There was something dark that came running for me in those woods. For years, it fed upon scraps and bones, but

34

when it smelled me," he laughed, "I was too delicious to pass up and so came the Wendigo, and it wanted to eat me up whole."

"It ripped open my muscles and scratched at my bones." He touched an old scar along his arm, "I still carry the scars from the attack, even all these years later."

"When I was nearly dead and dying, it offered me a choice and now, I'm offering that choice to you."

"What choice would that be?" Emmaline asked, surprising herself with the sound of her own voice.

"I'm offering you the choice to become a Wendigo like me, or test your fate to the systems in a game that's not meant to help you."

"You're hungry for wealth," he said with a sniff, "I can smell it in your heart. You crave to be near it, but you do not possess it yourself." He stood up and walked over to her and let his hand linger on her arm.

"I smelled it upon you when I returned to the city and brought brutal winter with me," He removed his jacket and began unbuttoning his shirt.

"You brought me here. You called to me like I called to the Wendigo who made me so long ago."

Where his torso should have been, was instead a collection of decomposing and molding bones, sticks, moss, and cobwebs. Together they formed a rotted ribcage that looked like the winter forest floor. At the center of his chest, was a heart made of ice. Frozen veins held it in place like an icy spider's web. The illusion of his manhood melted away and instead he was a decaying skeleton held together with moss and bone, still living by a curse set long ago.

"If you refuse," he said, "you will be destroyed by her family and their lawyers so fast you won't even know what hit you. She's from one of the wealthiest families in the city and you're just a little nobody. Who would believe your intentions were pure? I don't even think you believe that of yourself."

"I didn't mean for any of this to happen." Emmaline said softly. She was what he said she was. She was a nobody who was now surrounded by the death of the two people she relied upon for a lifestyle she could not call her own. Had she wanted too much from them?

"With me by your side," he said, "a rich and powerful man of the city, of the world, I can protect you. I can save you from this. You can belong to me in my home." He reached into his chest and pulled out his heart of ice.

Emmaline looked at the still and frosted heart. Claire's death would be blamed on her and maybe even Grace's too. Was she so innocent, she wondered?

The Wendigo offered her his frozen heart and she took it into her hands. There was no choice for Emmaline. Knowing what to do before she even knew it, Emmaline bit into the Wendigo's heart of ice.

Death hit her cold and fast. As Emmaline fell to the floor, she reached out for Claire's cold hand and let her guilt, remorse, and what was left of her warm heart flow into Claire's body. She let the memories of the two of them float out of her: running from the afternoon rain into the flea market, lounging in front the evening fires, and the afternoon when Claire dipped over to brush Adelaide's cheek with her lips and the two of them stopped talking after that. Emmaline knew it was all her fault and felt guilty for it all.

The pooled blood drew back into Claire's body.

"What are you doing?" The Wendigo demanded, sounding scared and out of control for the first time all night. "Stop it! Stop it now!"

When love has been uncorked, it's hard to put it back and Emmaline had finally let her heart open wide. Claire grew warm and moved. Her eyes fluttered open and when she saw Emmaline, she smiled. Emmaline could feel the warmth draining from her own body and into Claire's.

Emmaline felt chilled as a frost went through her, but she could feel her heart beating. Her hair became white like ice and her eyes a frosted grey. She was turning, but not into what the Wendigo had wanted, because a Wendigo feels no love, nor remorse, but she was not Wendigo.

She was born of the cold winter, but like the tree in the depths of the deepest frost, her heart was not frozen as his had been. Like the first blossom of Spring, Emmaline was born anew.

The Heath Estate

The air was still inside the vast estate, but just outside, winter's howling winds bounced and tumbled like an invisible force against the windows of the halls and rooms. Adelaide felt the house's resistance to the outside world—it's *rejection* of it. Crossing the threshold held such an overwhelming experience of otherness that Adelaide could not move herself farther into the estate, but instead remained just inside, peering out at the wild landscape.

The woods were wet with crumbling leaves poking out from underneath patches of snow still dotted with the early morning tracks of animals. Thick bunches of moss clung to boulders. Icicles hung low on veined rock faces. Heavy clouds lined the sky like a down comforter.

The estate stood alone on the high cliffs above the Hudson River. Adelaide checked her phone again: no messages, no calls, and no voicemails. No one was coming. Adelaide turned it off and slipped the phone into her jacket, rather carelessly. She shook off the loneliness that washed over her. After all, she thought, this was a place where people had once lived with the richness and fullness of a gilded life, and in the warmer months, the house was filled with tourists and visitors. If there was joy and warmth here once, then perhaps she could find it again on this cold winter's night.

Dark wings fluttered past the window in her periphery. When she turned to look, it was gone. All that remained was the stark landscape against the growing blizzard. Adelaide watched as the first snowflakes fell. They looked so innocent (such small things floating down from the sky) but in force they were dangerous, deadly even. Adelaide locked the heavy door behind her. She wasn't sure who or what she was keeping out, but it brought her an artificial sense of safety. Because of course, she wasn't safe. She was alone in the growing storm.

As Adelaide ventured into the house, she ran her hands against the worn velvet of the chairs and chaises that lined the hall. She tried to feel the warmth of those who had once sat here for tête-à-têtes, whispered promises, or a moment's reprieve. She wondered if her touch could activate an osmosis of these past lives into the present. If she could run her hands over the objects of the past and ponder them in just the right way . . . but it was a silly thought, she told herself as she flicked on the lights.

The light grew, faint at first, but then held steady at a faint faerie glow. Etched crystal bulbs with gold sconces lined the walls like torches to a tomb. She paused to examine her reflection in an impressive gold-leafed mirror. There was a certain haggardness that haunted her thin frame, but now in the smudged reflection of the mirror she looked downright skeletal. She tried to smooth her dark hair, but to no lasting effect. Adelaide poked and prodded at herself, until she gave up with a defeated sigh. She had hoped for a more dignified entrance into the estate. The place had always made her feel as if she should be presented at her best. This was not it.

Adelaide couldn't help but think dark thoughts about the whole mess. Only after she arrived at the noticeably empty estate, did she realize no one else was there to help her. Surely someone must be coming, she thought, though no one arrived.

She had ignored all the blizzard warnings and went up on the day circled in her calendar without talking to anyone. Weeks could go by like that for her. Adelaide enjoyed the silence winter brought her. She would say she was working on a book about the estate and some of the folk lore in the area, but really, she was just indulging herself. She opened bottles of wine at three in the afternoon, made herself extravagant lunches, and curled herself around the wood fire that burned brightly all throughout the day.

Adelaide and the estate both hibernated. Winter was always a time of dreams and half-dreams. Dreams that lingered upon waking to a cold and grey morning, pushing Adelaide to retreat once more to bed. After a season of this, the lines between waking and dreaming were blurred more and more for Adelaide. Her dreams haunted her well into midday, lingering just outside of her vision. The first hour of the morning was the worst of all. Shifting through showers and cups of coffee, she was like the walking dead: enticed by one world, reluctantly tied to the other. No matter the dream, it haunted her.

She had always felt called to the estate, like an invisible force pressing against her. It had become more and more demanding of her—*insistent* even. Their moods were so linked that she had grown as sullen and quiet as the closed estate. They had both become lonely in the long dark days of winter. She wasn't surprised that she had come up without any regard to the weather. The two of them kept their appointments with each other.

Now, as she walked through the house, Adelaide was preoccupied with a thought that had begun as a small itch at the back of her mind and was now clawing its way to the front. If she had any hope of independence from the house, it was crushed by the intimacy of solitude. She had been alone in the house before, but the blizzard left her helpless to its generosity. It was her only lifeline, and the estate was not known for its warmth.

Adelaide ran her hands along the walls where a faint layer of dust formed from months of neglect. A sudden bang erupted from underneath her touch. She pulled her hand away from the wall and shook her head at her skittishness. The house had a rudimentary heating system in place, something with radiators and boilers to make sure the pipes didn't freeze. Adelaide never bothered to learn how it all worked. Knocking and banging were common occurrences, but it startled her all the same. To her, it was an ominous sound, like the heartbeat of the house, sputtering to life.

She shifted her overnight bag from one shoulder to the other. She hadn't brought much with her, just a few necessities to get her through a couple days of uninterrupted work. A significant majority of the space was taken up by the manuscript and extensive notes for her book on the estate and local legends. Holding it gave her a sense of authority that she felt she lacked otherwise. She had brought it to work on in the evenings, when distractions would be limited and she could force herself, through the prospect of sheer boredom, to get some work done. After all, the house wouldn't open again for another month.

Adelaide needed the time to carefully comb over the artifacts to create new and interesting exhibitions to draw visitors to the house. There were other, more famous and subsequently more interesting, estates in the area. The Heath Estate was only just dragging along in the competition. The estate was often a consolation prize for brides on popular wedding dates, families looking to duck the long lines elsewhere, or dreamers entranced by the solitude of the house. Even the staff took on their roles reluctantly, often hoping it would provide a spring board to some better opportunity, but not Adelaide.

As a lover of strange things, Adelaide had grown fond of the estate at a young age. Her mother had too. The two of them would make the short drive from the small neighboring town where they lived and take long slow walks around the house, pretending it was theirs. They sat on the lawn, unwrapping their peanut butter sandwiches and pouring thermoses of lemonade as if they were the most delicious things in the world. That was the magic of the place for Adelaide.

Adelaide's mother passed away slowly, each day leaving her with a little less life. She had been dying for well over a decade, as if deciding to stay or not and never quite making up her mind. Her illness set in after Adelaide's father abandoned the family for another woman. He explained to the two of them that it would be better for everyone if they just all moved on with their lives. "Start fresh," were the words he used after they had finished their pieces of cake that her mother made for Adelaide's sixteenth birthday. After all the shouting and breaking of things, Adelaide and her mother made a silent pact—it would be the two of them until the end. The end, it seemed, came much faster for her mother than Adelaide expected.

Adelaide wandered into the dining room. She ran her hand over the smooth mahogany dining table, imagining the extravagant dinners that had been served upon it. At the far end of the room there was a massive fireplace with three panels above it depicting a medieval hunting scene: men chasing down a boar, killing it, and carrying its cadaver to roast. In the corner stood a large organ, hungry for someone to shake the dust from its rusty pipes.

She tucked herself behind a discreet side entrance to the room and arrived at the top of a clean, yet practical, spiral staircase. The estate had several such hidden staircases, so that the household staff of the era could carry out their tasks without being seen. She thrust her hand into the darkness, feeling around the wall for the switch. A string of bare lightbulbs lit up the stairwell. The plain wooden walls of the staircase were a sharp contrast to the carved oaks and mahoganies of the dining room. Adelaide wondered about the people who had walked these staircases in the shadows of the house. Would they have felt the two worlds under one roof?

Adelaide walked down the stairs toward the kitchen. Unlike the rest of the house, the kitchen was equipped with modern appliances like stainless steel refrigerators and a ten-burner gas stove. The estate had updated it for catering companies to use when wealthy patrons from the city rented the house for private events. In the remodel, the designer knocked down an old wall and, in its place, installed large windows that overlooked the river.

Adelaide watched as the newly fallen snow blanketed the earth and covered the pock marks that formed in the warmth of daylight. Everything was flush with white. Snowflakes fell lackadaisically in the wind, blowing this way and that. If Adelaide had not been standing, she would not have known which way was up or down. The world before her faded into a pale blue as the sun set and became darker inch by inch.

She fiddled around the cabinets, looking for a kettle and the bottle of bourbon she had stashed just as the season ended. Adelaide found both easily. She made it a point to be the last person in the house at the end of the season, looking over everything and locking up doors. There were more qualified people to do the job, but no one enjoyed it as much as she did. She loved knowing that she would be the last one out and the first one in, year in and year out, as if the place was her own.

Everything in the kitchen was packaged in single servings. A steady stream of parties had a way of shaping a kitchen like that. Adelaide rummaged through packets of honey and tea bags (no doubt left over from the tea service of a wedding or a boozy brunch) and poured the ingredients together into a warm drink. It wasn't champagne, but it would do. She imagined it was the kind of drink a cook would have made when Edgar Heath roamed the halls of his estate.

Adelaide could imagine such a cook, just over there by the fireplace, sitting with her feet against the dying fire and a warm mug in her hands. Adelaide wanted to press her hands through the veil of time and hear the house come alive with the sounds of the past. She closed her eyes, imagining the soft brush of feet against the floor as the last of the staff snuffed out the last of the fires in the fireplaces. She could hear the gentle clatter of the last of the pots being scrubbed and placed to dry. Another day of chaos in the kitchen culled into the quiet din of cleanliness and tidiness, only to be repeated once more the next day and the next.

A bang from behind the wall startled Adelaide from her day dream. The sound curled around the room, like an unseen bird hovering overhead, before bouncing up through the ceiling and disappearing into a cloud of silence. At times, Adelaide felt as if the house spoke directly to her. The shine of the setting sun on the ballroom floor was romance and poetry. The summer breeze on the terrace was a love note. The hissing of pipes was an offer to play and romp. And now, the wind whistling against the windows was a warning. Adelaide was sure of that.

After a quick rummage through the freezer and pantry, Adelaide had assuaged her fears. The house was strong. It had held against storms before and it would hold again. The kettle and oven hummed away happily in the heat. Warmth from the kitchen spilled into the neighboring spaces. Already, the house was waking up from its long winter's nap. Rows of pastry puffs stuffed with savory fillings, mini quiches, spanakopita, and canapes lined the cooking sheets Adelaide pulled out of the oven. They were the leftovers of parties past, all stored away and forgotten by everyone but Adelaide. She felt as if she were resurrecting each party with each frozen delight that was reheated.

A tray of quiches brought to life the summer revelers from the wedding party on the lawn, where a jazz band played under twinkling lights. The puff pastries summoned the family reunion where hordes of children zoomed around the long halls, chasing each other until they had all fallen to the ground utterly exhausted and deliriously happy. Canapes revived the corporate event in late spring, where Adelaide spied upon a young couple in the back of a presentation holding hands when they thought no one was watching. Adelaide could feel them all now, unbounded by the laws of time.

A light fog formed along the windows from the heat and movement of the kitchen. Adelaide felt like she was inside the mouth of the estate. As it came alive, its mouth breathed upon the glass in thick and heavy exhalations. Bourbon continued to flow as Adelaide consumed piping hot hors devours straight from the oven. She abandoned her coat after her second mug. Her cheeks felt flush and her head spun.

The snow was streaming down in fat heavy flakes. In her loosened and careless state, she began to rummage through the drawers and cabinets aimlessly. Adelaide had rather gotten into the habit when she first returned to the house to check that everything was in its place. Things had a way of moving in a large estate with so many people passing through, so she found it a comfort to be able to place her hands upon things and know that they were there.

She rifled through a loose stack of papers in a forgotten corner of the countertop. Flipping through its contents, she found an old beaten-up brochure and unfolded its tattered pages to a rough map of the estate. She touched the tip of her finger to the dark ink against the yellowing paper. Long sure lines followed the length of the house where it bordered the edge of the cliff. The spiraling of the staircases made her dizzy as she followed their descent through the halls of the house.

Against the paper, the house looked like a labyrinth. As a curator, Adelaide saw the house as a collection of time, of people, and of their stories. All of them compiled and compressed on top of one another. They were all looped together and only separated by the perception of linearity. In her work, Adelaide was given the rare chance to see past that separation in the collection of artifacts across eras. To her they existed simultaneously.

Quite satisfied with the state of the kitchen's inventory, and full from her scrounged dinner and bourbon, Adelaide gathered her things. She had an aching desire to curl up and wait out the storm somewhere more intimate. The largeness of the house always drove her to seek out small places. Adelaide's favorite spot was her office at the uppermost floor of the house, where previous members of the household staff had once lived. These days it was used for storage, which suited Adelaide's needs just fine. While Adelaide called it an office, it was really just one of the old bedrooms she cleared out and had set up an old desk next to a rusty cot.

She returned to the spiral staircase and looked upward past all four floors of the house. The ascent was never easy. Her breath puffed heavy from her chest and her blood moved hot and fast through her body. In the repetition of stairs, she lost her sense of time. To her it seemed as if all there was, and ever would be, were white stairs. Be it some combination of bourbon or lethargy, Adelaide began to experience waves of light headedness, and would suddenly feel like she was falling down the white stairs like a snowflake in the storm, then in the next moment, she would find herself perfectly upright. It was as if her time had been split in two, where she was both in perpetual free fall and forward motion simultaneously.

The spell was broken when she arrived to the very top. Adelaide steadied herself at the top of the landing and peered out from the lit stairway into the darkness of the hall. Light had a strange way of moving in the house. The vintage glass of the windows gave the twilight a twisted look, forever held in perpetual refraction. Up here, on the topmost floor, the windows let the light come in and play, even in the darkest of nights. As her eyes adjusted, she took a moment longer to look down the hallway. There was never darkness up here. Perhaps that's why she preferred it.

A quick flick of the switch was all it took to dissipate the strange and silent world. Bright bulbs lined the long hallway filled with doors: six on one side and six on the other. Adelaide's little office was at the very end of the hallway, as far as she could get from everyone else. Spending the night was not a common occurrence for the current staff of the estate, but everyone made an exception for Adelaide. Not because they found her behavior strange or improper, but because they simply couldn't be bothered to give her whereabouts a second thought. It was how she, and everyone else, preferred it.

A swift shoulder nudge to the door and she was inside. Adelaide plopped her bag onto her desk and herself onto the cot. She watched as shadows curled and pressed against the ceiling in endless loops. She was still dizzy and breathless from the bourbon. She closed her eyes and let herself fall back in time.

From the far corner of the room, she followed the hem of a maid's dress as she walked out of the room and down the hallway. Pairs of feet crisscrossed one another as they made their way through the halls, down the invisible staircases, and into the grand bedrooms of the estate. Their prospective persons were like ghosts, flitting in and out, silent and unseen. The house was alive with pathways, always in motion like the intricate parts of a large machine that operated like a living thing.

When she opened her eyes, the overwhelming emptiness of the large estate returned. The storm beat against the sides of house like an angry mob. Violent winds rushed past like screams in the night. Enough creaks and groans issued from the walls let her know the house was still resisting, but each one sounded less resolved than the last. Adelaide turned and felt for the cord of her desk lamp, like she had so many times before. A soft and easy glow lit the room. Adelaide stretched out on the bed once more, willing herself to rise.

A sudden bang at the end of the hall startled her to sitting. The sound bounded through the walls and disappeared. Adelaide had half begun to entertain the thought that the sound was following her through the house. Somehow, she found it reassuring, as if reminding her she wasn't alone. The house was there for her, reaching out and trying to hold her in the only way it could.

With the prospect of an empty evening ahead of her, Adelaide turned towards the loose stacks of paper she had thrown in her bag. Work would be a welcome tonic against the boredom of the evening. She wrote freehand of course, transcribing her notes to text when she found the time. At first, she tried using only inked lines and typewritten pages. The idea of using the instruments of the past to bring them into the present was poetic, charming, and alchemical. After losing several versions due to wine stains, open fires, and a general lack of personal organization, she acquiesced to the era of the computer, begrudgingly and spiteful.

Adelaide hoped it would be the kind of book that would be sold in the gift shop of the estate and local establishments. She so badly wanted to see her name attached to something that she could hold—as if to say, *yes, I did exist.* In all truth, she was no great writer. Her work tended to rely on the dramatic and the flair for the supernatural that was so popular. Any historian worth their salt would reject her work in an instant, but that wasn't who she was trying to impress anyway. She wrote so that the present may have a direct link to the past—and might thereby by pulled through to the present. It was a yearning to not let it waste away in obscurity, but to hold tightly to the past and all its members. She was performing a resurrection with each brush stroke of her pen.

In the soft-lit room, she shifted her pages to the very beginning. These pages had become stained and soft from her reading them so often. Every time she began, she had to go back to the beginning in order to understand where she was in the present. This was a crucial part of her process, but often kept her blocked and stalled. Every time she began her work, she began by reading the same words:

Built from the imagination of a man trapped in the confines of having too much, the Heath Estate mirrors Edgar Heath's madness for consumption. Too large, too loud, too inappropriate, the building rests on the outskirts of acceptable society in structure and morality. The Heath family fortune was rumored to have been accrued by ill-gotten means; whether by double crossing a partner in a steel transaction, or by a manipulation of stocks and bonds. There was no doubt that the reputation of the family was disreputable to say the least. What is more unknown is who, or what, haunts the estate, and how long it has been haunted.

One theory is that the place resides on a sentient energy that was, and still is, unaware of the passage of time as it sits in a space that could be occupied by anything. Another theory suggests that ancient spirits haunt the high cliffs where the house was built. Reports of unearthly screams have been documented there for hundreds of years, beginning with accounts from fishermen and boatmen that sailed past those insurmountable crags when the town was still a Dutch trading outpost.

Still, others suggested that Edgar's wife, Rosemera, dark beauty that she was, haunts the halls in death as she had in life. Restricted to a wheelchair for inexplicable medical reasons, be it her own incurable misery, Rosemera hadn't set foot outside of the house in years. She was found dead one winter morning with smoke still steaming from her lungs as if she had died by a terrible fire, when there had been none. Stranger still, at the moment of death, she took her bedding and wrapped it over herself, forever encasing herself in her own odd tomb.

Then of course, there is the spirit of Edgar Heath himself. This is the most prevalent and accepted theory of who, or what, haunts the Heath estate. His death was even more mysterious than his wife's. In 1902, an unsuspecting gardener who was planting bulbs for spring, found the

*decaying body of Edgar in the frosted ground of the flower
bed. Except for the fact that he was dead, the coroner couldn't
find any medical rationale for his death. It was as if Edgar
had laid down in the cold to die.*

*When questioned by the police, the staff, even more
perplexed than the authorities, assured them that they heard
their employer's footsteps in the small bedroom where he
became more and more withdrawn. He hardly ate, slept, or
even spoke. One housekeeper swore that she received daily
communications from Edgar himself in regard to the
household payments and expenses. The poor woman, so
distraught by these turns of events, spent the rest of her life
within walking distance of the town's doctor and insisted on
daily appointments until her death.*

Adelaide paused. Sounds of shuffling echoed from the
down the hall. She tipped her chair for a quick peek. There
was nothing she could see. Adelaide was not one to fear
strange noises. She rose in search of the loose shutter or
wayward critter trapped inside the house. They were common
enough in a place as large and old as the estate. Things came
unhinged. Creatures came inside. People were always in and
out of the place. Nothing was ever really still.

Adelaide opened each door to investigate, but nothing
was out of place amongst the boxes and folded chairs. As she
moved through the rooms, she lifted lids at random and moved
things around without rhyme or reason. Her hands stayed
busy, but her mind wandered. The time that passed between
the seasons made everything seem strange and foreign to her.
She rifled through things, trying to recall when she had last
seen them. What started as a hunt, became a kind of inventory
check as Adelaide looked through the things that had been
stored. She found herself getting caught up in the minutiae of
the modern event stemware and chargers, which were in direct
contrast to the estate's collections of silver candlesticks and
brass hand bells.

Adelaide had become so engrossed in looking through
boxes that she forgot entirely about the source of her search.
She was picking her way through a collection of old photos

when she heard the distinct creak of the door closing behind her. Out of her periphery, a shadow slipped past the door frame. With a quick turn on her heel, she leapt toward it. A bang from the wall beside her made her jump and scream. It was nothing. There was nothing. She shook her head.

When she turned toward the boxes once more, the slam of a door made her spin around sharply. She knew exactly where to look and ran down the hall. With a force much stronger than she needed, she threw open the door to the stairwell. Standing at the top, she could hear someone moving down the stairs, and quickly.

Adelaide followed them, taking the stairs two at a time. Whoever it was must have been squatting in the house for the winter, or was perhaps a lost traveler in the storm. The footsteps exited the stairway on the floor below. Adelaide wasn't even sure what she would do if and when she finally caught the invisible intruder. Chasing them down gave her the sense that she was in control. Standing still was no longer an option. She mustered her courage and cracked open the door just enough to see out into the hallway. Adelaide shook at what she saw.

The lights had been turned on and the hallway was glistening. Every handle, doorknob, and each little thing made of brass had a bright sheen and polish as if an invisible butler had gone round on orders from Edgar Heath to give the place a quick shine. Adelaide reasoned with herself that there had to be an explanation: someone came up early to prepare the house before the storm. Perhaps, the intruder was another one of the estate's staff, stranded like her. It was a large house with many places to wander and still never know what was happening just on the other side.

On this floor alone, there were a dozen bedrooms, but the two at each end were the largest. They were the bedrooms of Edgar Heath and Rosemera. Between them were ten rooms that Edgar Heath had created for visiting guests, but even during the estate's golden hour, very few ever came to stay. There was nothing but empty space between the two.

One by one, she began to go through the rooms. She kept herself cool headed through force of will. Her heart was beating furiously. Outside, she could hear the intensity of the storm grow. The house would hold, she told herself. The banging from the winds grew stronger and with it, the house's resistance. Even the wallpaper seemed to be screaming. Every beat and breath of the house was fighting to keep the lines intact.

The smaller bedrooms were cold and dark. Adelaide had converted the majority of the rooms into exhibits about the history of the estate. In the shadows, they seemed strange and foreign to her. Had she placed the iron tools of the builders like that? Had the exhibit of flower pressings somehow shifted over the season? Were those her words on the signage? Her questions were met with silence. There was no one.

Except, she had the very strange feeling that she was moving concurrent to someone else. When she entered a room, she felt as if someone only just left it. She looked for clues as to the stranger's whereabouts, but found nothing. It was as if they vanished. Adelaide opened the door to Edgar Heath's bedroom.

Lights flickered against the dark blue wallpaper with tight black patterns. The room adjacent to the hallway was a sitting room that proceeded the bedroom itself. Adelaide fashioned it to resemble how it looked when Edgar Heath was alive. Unlike the other rooms, she staged it so that it gave visitors the impression that Edgar Heath could walk in at any moment. There was a half-penned letter on the desk and a pair of reading glasses perched atop a book in the chair next to the fireplace. What were once charming anecdotes in the light of a summer's day, now seemed ominous and threatening. If there was an intruder, this was the room with the most evidence for it. Only, Adelaide was the one who had put those things there.

A bang erupted above her head. Instead of retreating elsewhere, the sound stayed, bouncing in and around the walls of the room. Bangs ranging from soft knocks to loud explosions erupted in a cacophony of sound. Adelaide covered her ears with her hands. A violent crashing from the bedroom beyond forced her to retreat into the hall.

The very foundations of the house rattled beneath her. Another loud and violent crash from Edgar Heath's room resounded. Adelaide turned and ran towards the end of the hall—as far away as she could think to get. She flung herself into Rosemera's sitting room, locking the door behind her. Bangs, hisses, and groans echoed down the hall. Smoke wafted towards her. The house had fallen.

The door to Rosemera's bedroom was open, as if the woman herself was calling to Adelaide and welcoming her into the intimate space. She passed through the sitting room decorated with golds and emeralds. Where Edgar Heath's room was all business, Rosemera's was filled with little luxuries. Small instruments and poofs had been scattered along the edges of the room. Heavy velvet drapes with gold cording lined the walls. On side tables, large bell jars entombed birds' nests with moss and feathers.

Adelaide recalled the moment when she began placing the objects in the room in such a way that wasn't necessarily accurate to the time period. It was instead, how her mother had kept her room. Emboldened by the unresponsiveness of the exhibit's viewers to the changes, Adelaide had even begun to place her mother's objects in Rosemera's bedroom. The two women were forever linked in her mind—right down to the dusty wheelchair that clung to the shadows in both of their rooms.

The walls shook and swayed. Popping and hissing sounds resounded all around her. She could feel the fire crawling through the walls as if it were crawling through her own veins. Adelaide retreated to the bed and curled herself into the musty sheets. Smoke pushed out from underneath the door and filled the room. Adelaide lifted the sheets above her head, as if that alone could ward off the inevitable. The breaking of things resounded all around her. The house crashed and crumbled in the fires below and the violent winds above. A quick and loud explosion resounded and a furious wave of fire rushed upward. Adelaide felt herself falling. Surely, she thought, someone must be coming.

The World Walker of Central Park

*"Nil igitur mors est ad nos neque pertinent hilum
quandoquidem natura animi mortalis habetur."*
~Lucretius

The infestation began one night in late May as I was
dreaming of the leaves falling in my hand. I awoke with an
unknown terror, mumbling something about "dead and dried
leaves in my hand" to my dream-dewed and semi-conscious
spouse beside me. When I came to my senses, I turned over
the pillow and there underneath, was the cockroach.

By summer's end, cockroaches invaded our home. We
assumed that they were slipping through the cracks of the
walls and crawling down from the chimney, but they were
almost supernatural in their ability to appear out of nothing
from seemingly nowhere. I started to see them crawling in the
shadows, even when the flip of a light switch revealed
otherwise. Each night before bed, I would vacuum and
rearrange the furniture, as if I were trying to trick ghosts. Still,
they came.

I was a peaceful person by nature, but with these
creatures I became a ruthless killer. Even after I discovered the
alarming knowledge that cockroaches expressed distinct
personality types, I did not stall my slapping and killing, but
instead, made it a quick death out of some guilt or desire to be
merciful.

Poison was not an option for us. We were trying,
unsuccessfully, to have a baby. Plastics were all but banned
entirely from the household, and anything remotely toxic was
out of the question. When the leaves began to fall in October,
the cockroaches disappeared as quickly and quietly as they
had arrived.

One late Saturday autumn afternoon, we returned from
a particularly stressful doctor's appointment that had left my
partner distraught upon our arrival home. I went out under the
pretext of getting our favorite cross-town takeout (that after
decades of service still refused to deliver) as a treat to try and

raise our spirits. Really though, I needed the air. It felt cruel to leave, but I could tell I had already begun to make the situation worse. My humor was too dark, and all my good intentions were for nothing. I wasn't the one who wanted a child.

I couldn't begin to imagine myself in the sacred covenant of parenthood. To bring life into the world felt like an enormous spiritual task, which I did not feel ready for in the slightest. I secretly rejoiced in our failings. To pull a living thing from the ether of creation felt as sinister to me as a life being drawn back into it. I could only see darkness in it all.

The day was still cold and grey with low hanging clouds, making the transition to evening especially quiet and eerie. Leaves fell and the wind drew them up around me in tight circles. I made my way up a winding path towards the peak of a summit, where plays, impromptu performances, and weddings were often held. At night, it became a gathering place. The brief moments when it was empty were my favorite. I could find solitude without loneliness, as if the constant presence of the others who frequented the spot were never gone far from it.

As I ventured upwards, a feather on the ground caught my eye. Farther ahead, I saw another, then another until there was a whole clump. There was no blood, but there was also decidedly no bird, not living at least.

"Must've been beautiful." A voice said up ahead.

"Yeah. Shame." I replied.

I turned to the man on the bench just ahead. My walks in the park conditioned me to expect a stranger to strike up a conversation. Hell, all of New York did that for me. Everyone was always in conversation with the next person.

He was small with a tight build. I would have picked him for an old boxing champ, or maybe a jockey. I could never tell with sports.

"Saw the poor thing on my way here," he said as he motioned to the bench he sat upon, "Can't help but feel sorry for a thing like that."

"It's terrible—frightening almost," I said.

"I once saw something like that happen," he said as he drank from a tall can of ice tea, the kind from the corner bodega. "A hawk came down and, *thwap*," he said with a clap of his hands, "little birdie was gone in an instant."

"That's horrifying!"

"Are you horrified by death?"

"Who isn't?" I shrugged.

"Are you horrified by life?"

"Life?" I turned to look him directly in the eye. It was the kind of question that seemed too specific, and yet, I had never seen this man before—had I? "What kind of life are you talking about?"

"The kind of bringing-into-the-world life," he said with a slight smile.

"And how would you know that?"

"You don't remember me?" He asked.

"Okay. I think I'm done," with a curt wave.

"You didn't come when I sent them," he said, "I thought you would, but you didn't."

"Sent what?"

"My messengers! They guide in the dark. The ancient creatures that show you the way."

"You can't mean . . . the cockroaches?"

"Yeah! So, you got the message. Why didn't you come?"

"How was I supposed to know that?"

"I took you to be a person of spirit," he said as he took a sip from his can. "Maybe I was wrong." He shrugged.

"Here," he pointed over to the bird feathers beside the path.

I followed his gaze and to my bewilderment, the ghost of the songbird began to rise from the fallen feathers, fully formed, but not quite solid, as if it had been made of smoke.

"A dead songbird to show us the way," he said. "If you're willing?

"The way to where?"

"To the world of the dead."

"Right," I said a bit too smug, "and, ah, how do we get there exactly?"

"Our songbird knows the way."

We followed the bird to a large boulder that rose out of the ground. I had always thought there was something a bit spooky about this spot. Like a guard at post, a honey locust tree, with thorns as thick as knitting needles wrapped in bunches around its bark, stood on top of the boulder.

"Ah, hm," he said as he pointed to the needles. "If you could just prick your finger here and we can be on our way."

"Blood as the key? Seems cliché, doesn't it?"

He shrugged. "Myths gotta start from somewhere, right? Besides, you come into this life covered in blood and go out the same way. Makes sense you need to bleed a little to get in again."

I pressed the tip of my finger against the sharp thorn until it bled. With my finger bloodied I look back for direction. Our spirit songbird had perched itself on the thorn where I had pricked my finger and peered down at me with a curious tilt of its head.

"Give it a little shake on the rock," my guide said.

"Doesn't that seem a little . . . informal?"

"Psh," he waved away my concern, "ritual is far less formal than you urbanites think. Remember, I knew your ancestors. They weren't exactly the sophisticates you all pretend to be!"

I felt foolish and somewhat reluctantly shook my finger until tiny drops of blood fell on the stone. Like a hurricane spinning in the sea, the rock and the earth began to swirl until in the center of it all an opening appeared. The bird slipped through first, my guide second, and I—taking one last look backwards—followed them.

I was set by some unknown hand upon a humble dirt path. Roots and bones poked out of the earth like bushes. Empty carcasses of bugs and the skeletons of birds skirted past in the tattered grasses and rotting leaves. As I watched, a stream of cockroaches with crushed bodies scattered past. I flinched at the harm that I had no doubt caused them and their brothers.

I gasped at the wild nature spirits from the fables of my childhood that joined in the reverie of this underground park. Some were small and stilted with mushrooms growing from their skins and patches of lichen covering their bodies. Others seemed almost human-like on two legs with two arms carrying baskets of collected sticks and bones or rotting food. There were spirits of mushrooms, spawning like spores and then reforming themselves over and over like a fast-moving loop. Some seemed to be comprised of part fish, half bivalve, or three-quarters oyster. There was something of a river quality to these spirits, even in the way they moved and slipped through the crowds.

A woman covered in dirt and the rotting filth of the earth walked past me. I thought she might have been made of mud at some point. She wore what I interpreted as an old Victorian dress that was tattered and torn. Her bustle was like the kind of mushroom poof I had popped as a child. Creatures of slime followed in her wake: frogs, snails, worms, and others far more gruesome and ancient in origin that I could not place were also in her train. She walked past with a grunt and seemed almost to pay me no mind.

"The mistress of dirt and filth," my guide announced with a bow as she walked past like royalty. "Your ancient human ancestor."

We walked a mirror image of the very path I had taken aboveground. Above us was a darkened sky lit by a shadowed moon, and yet everything was illuminated in a ghostly light. Squirrel carcasses raced up trees with missing tails. Birds perched on top of tree limbs with splintered wings. Insects with legs and chunks missing from their bodies crawled across the leaves. Spirits of trees past rustled their branches in an invisible wind.

"This world is a mirror image of the one below us," my guide said as he picked up the can of ice tea he had discarded earlier. Down here it was full once more. "This world is beneath you just as you are beneath it—twin images sort of thing," he said with a crack of the can. "Cheers," (I had the inclination that perhaps it held a spirit stronger than ice tea.) Our songbird circled and glided above us with a sweet song goodbye.

Outside the park, tall buildings mirrored the ones above us. Only down here, a building was a composite not just of the buildings I knew, but of the buildings that had come before them too. There were wooden houses crunched on the base of apartment buildings and brownstones mashed in between slick glass sides. Untold varieties of building types had been slapped, smooshed, and scrunched together.

People passed us in all centuries of garbs and garments. Each person wore their death upon them without a care or concern. The smashed head was still smashed. The disease that had spread upon them and closed their lives was still living on their skin. Even pieces of pitchforks, metal rods, and a variety of everyday objects jutted out from heads and bodies. When their persons walked, the impaled objects bobbed along in step with them.

Those who were once enemies, shook hands and gave bows in a far more friendly manner than they had known above the earth. Groups of seemingly disparate peoples gathered on the street corners, under building vestibules, and along benches. The poor, the rich, the outcast, the socialites, the thieves, and the holy men of all centuries made merry together.

Scenes of a more domestic nature occupied the grand apartment buildings along the park. From my view on the ghostly sidewalk, I could see groups gathered around crowded dinner tables, engaged in cocktail conversations in living rooms, and entertained by all manner of frivolity in bedrooms. The city itself seemed more populated and packed than it was above ground, but there was no sense of the competitive nature in regard to space and materials. The delineation of self that is so carefully maintained in life, seemed not to matter a bit in death.

"Let's drop in for a drink somewhere," my guide said as he tossed his empty can to the ground. "I know a spot that's good."

His habit of littering, which had previously annoyed me, made more sense as a sociably acceptable practice in this locale. The ground was covered in a crust of trash and discarded objects that had been accumulating for centuries. Long pieces of old construction materials, tire irons, and even the rare busted water tower broke out of the surfaces like trees in the road.

We padded upon the trash roads with a steady beat. Our pleasantries were an exchange of observation ("What does this do?") and explanation ("No one would drink that here!"). For there was something to discuss every other step it seemed. Emptiness was unknown here. Everywhere I looked something or someone filled the space. The city wasn't just filled with the deceased, but also failed businesses and forgotten fads. Anything that had died in the physical or proverbial found its way to this city beneath a city.

For a solitary character such as myself, I was astonished at how crowded and busy the life afterlife appeared. Loneliness was unknown here. There was no exploitation of the ego nor any sense of solitary ownership of anything. The collective understanding—it seemed—was devoted to merriment and pleasantries.

Artists and creatives thrived in this place. A collective of builders created sculptures from the scavenged pieces of garbage and trash. Several painters along the park and streets created landscapes using flecks of dried paint and discarded palates. Poets preached from torn pages on the corners. Singers gathered to create ghostly melodies and harmonies (even if a few of them didn't have the full use of their mouths, throats, or lungs). There was a full production of a play being performed in the middle of the road with a whole cast of dancers and musicians who happily tooted and strummed away on broken instruments.

"Here," my guide said with a quick look and a hop across the street. "This is it."

I tagged along like a child, unsure of where to go or what to do. For there was no rhyme or rhythm to the streets. Broken carriages, bicycles, cars, and even the rare rider on horseback went this way and that through the streets. Pushing through the stream of traffic felt like foraging a strong downstream river. Of course, I thought as I narrowly dodged and motorcade, what would be the point of traffic laws when everything is already broken and everyone is already dead.

Music welcomed us before we even entered the bar. A jazz band played with such gusto that with each opening of the door, music escaped with a blaring force that caused the people passing by to cover their ears—or what was left of them. We entered just as a party of revelers peeled out of the door. The door swung a bit on its hinges and the doorknob felt slick against my hand. We were inside.

All of the instruments were broken in some way: the piano with its missing keys, the standup bass with a chunk ripped from its side, the drums with their bent symbols, and the horns with their twisted trunks. Missing or broken bits and pieces seemed not to matter at all. To compensate, each musician played in a kind of rascal manner, with little or no attention to decorum, taste, or even historical usage of the instruments. Instead, the musicians tooted and banged out music that flowed from a cacophony to a rough patch of melody and harmony then back again to the chaos of solos and riffs.

Oh, how they had the crowd moving! Everyone danced wildly to the music as it bounced around the walls. Liquid from drinks went flying this way and that as bodies boogied and jived. Howls and cheers erupted at the end of solos, whenever a drink spilled, or generally whenever it was found to be appropriate, which was often.

We wound our way back towards the bar and away from the music. The bar itself was a composite of—what I assumed—the bars that had been there before it. Mismatched pieces of wood, bar stools, and liquor shelves made it look and feel like the music that played just beside it. Deep carves of

62

names and graffiti pock-marked the bar's surface and there was a slick feeling to the worn-down wood.

"Whatcha having then?" My guide asked.

"I'm okay."

"You gotta try something."

The bartender walked over with a slow and casual walk. He had a gaping wound in his head, which he had embellished with bits of colorful broken glass from liquor bottles throughout the ages. He had created an homage not only to the brews of the past, but also to the missing chunk of his head.

"Two scotches," my guide said with a casual wave to the bartender and then a quick turn to me, "You'll like it. Everything's vintage down here."

Our bartender returned with a smudged bottle and two different shot glasses (one circa 1994 and the other 1904). He poured the scotch slowly with a wink to my guide. This was his drink, I gathered, and this was his bartender. The rehearsal of the dance between them felt practiced. Here, I was the intruder.

"To the city of the dead," my guide said as he handed me my drink.

"Quite a place," I said before taking a hesitant taste. With the sip came a burst of sea water and a memory that wasn't mine. The fleeting thought was of a sailor just in for a stopover. "What was that?" I asked with a shake of my head.

"The person who drank that." He said with a smile that turned into a quick frown. "Whoever drank this just ate an oyster," he said with a spit on the floor, "I hate oysters."

"Interesting," I said while inspecting the foggy glass. "Even the drinks are dead."

"Spirits love spirits," he said with a long drink. "Much better," he said with a pleasant roll of his eyes, "someone on the bank of the river at sunset."

"So, what does this all add up to?" I asked, choking down the memory of a late-night shot gone wrong.

"Meaning?"

63

"What's the point of all this?" I said with a motion around me, "You said you wanted to show *me*. Why?"

"Why anything?" He shrugged. "You? I dunno, maybe just the knowledge that there's life after life—and it ain't too bad."

I shrugged.

"That's not it, is it?" Then with a small shake of his head and a sigh, "I hope I didn't pick up the wrong person again." He looked over to me, "You are worried about bringing life into the world though—please say that's you."

"Yeah, that sounds about right."

"So, what's the hold up with the realizations? You aren't *inspired*?"

"It's just that," I looked around, "all I see here is the past, not the future."

"And that's what you're worried about?"

"What?"

"The future," he said.

"Well, yeah." I said, "The past is known and done. There's a comfort to that."

"This is the place where all things end," he said. "This is your future. What else could you possibly have to know?"

"The close present and further future," I replied. "I want to know if it's going to be worth it."

"What worth could you possibly not find in your own life?" He replied with a bit of a condescending look.

"I'm tired of this constant struggle," I said exasperated. "There's nowhere to rest in this place of being settled or not. There's only so long a person can take being stuck in doldrums."

"Why struggle?" He asked. "Look around you. Does anyone look like they're struggling?"

"Everyone's dead and done in the past," I replied. "That's not where I am." I took a long sip and choked on memory of a musty cigar in a dark room. "I'm in the place of the present and the near future, where nothing is settled or sure."

"Look," he said, "for someone like me—an immortal being—I don't really see time that way." He finished his drink with a long gulp and a burp. "Someone's first drink!"

"How do you see it then?" I asked as I finished mine as well (a memory of an easy early evening at an uptown bar).

"Cyclical," he said as he waved to his bartender and stood. "Seasons come and go. Life and death continue. I drink and I wait, and I wait and I drink."

"Are you waiting for something?" I said following suite.

"Someone, usually."

"To help them?"

"Sometimes."

"How do you know what to do?"

"I just know," he said. "It's all part of the cyclical balance for me. I can sense when something should shift or something should be done or undone." He gave a bashful shrug, "I'm a creature of nature and city, of the dead and undead, and of the mortal and immortal. Balance is my element."

"And you think something should shift within me to regain the balance of . . . something?"

"Yes!" he exclaimed with a clap of his hands and an exuberant smile. "You finally understand!"

He bounced off into the crowd and began to dance his way through with a renewed and invigorated energy. I had no choice but to follow him. He moved and swayed through the crowd, moving from one dancing partner to the next in a smooth musical number.

I bobbed along a bit uncomfortable. I wished for the kind of freedom to move and dance with abandon. Something in me felt bound and trapped. In some ways, I felt as if I were the ghost among the living. A hard and steady drumbeat began to pulse through the air. The carousers stomped their feet in time, undulated their spines, and popped their chests to the thundering beat. A hot and wild reverie had come upon the crowd. Yet, I was still unmoved. I sank to the back of the room, trying my best to be unseen.

To my annoyance, I was unlucky. A cat, who I assumed haunted the bar in life as it did in death, spotted me. The tabby uncurled itself from its position on a rafter and with the precision of an Olympic athlete, landed itself right next to me. Half of its body was sunken in from some blunt trauma (perhaps the very same rafter). In a gesture of friendly curiosity, the cat sniffed at my clothes before offering its paw to me as a sort of nice-to-meet-you handshake. I took its tiny paw with as much decorum as I could muster and gave it a friendly shake.

"Treats," my guide said as he came up next to me. "Handshake's a nice touch though," he said as he jammed his hand into his pockets and came up with a small treat, which the cat happily accepted.

"Is everywhere here this dirty?" I asked.

"What do you mean by dirty?"

"Like this," I said with a motion toward the heap of bar napkins and red straws that had piled up in the corner for what seemed like decades. "Is everywhere so cluttered or is messiness just a condition of death?"

He snapped his fingers, "I've got just the place for you, and I could use another drink."

Before I could object, he grabbed me by shoulders in a far too affable and boisterous manner that told me I had no choice. I gave a quick look back at the tabby cat as a kind of apology for leaving so abruptly. As the door closed behind us, I could have sworn the cat waved goodbye.

"It's too far to walk," he said as he ran to the curb with a sharp whistle.

A tall carriage halted with a jolt and a bit of a tumble. One of its wheels was missing and in its place was a rusted steel barrel surrounded by a thick carpet. The stains and smells that had once irked its owner were nothing compared to the ones that covered it now. Through the dark crust of crud from the city of the dead, I could just see the pattern of a curling willow branch.

"Need a lift?" The driver asked with a polite tip of his top hat.

A gloved hand pulled back the curtain of the carriage to reveal a group of very inimitable people. They peered at me with as much intense curiosity as I at them. Not only were they in disparate dress and status, but also from very different periods of the city itself. Most were missing appendages and if I wasn't mistaken, one of the passengers seemed to be missing a head. They were a collection of people who would have never met in life, but here they were fellow travelers. They gave us both a jovial wave, which my guide responded to with a polite bow and smile.

"Going downtown?" My guide asked with a friendly lean on the carriage.

"Going anywhere you like," the driver responded with an exuberance and cheerfulness.

"Cheers to that!" My guide turned to whisper into the horse's ear. In response it gave a quick little nod so small and unnoticeable that I almost missed it. With an extra spring in his step, he hopped next to the driver.

"Space in the front up here or you can squeeze your way back there of you like—it's a bit tight, I'll warn you!" The driver said with a laugh.

"I'll take the front, thanks." I said as I hopped into the seat next to him.

The pair of horses were in far better shape than the carriage. They were both large and quite dark in appearance. With a quick click of the driver's tongue, they were off bouncing through the streets at a clip that was both joyous to them and terrifying to me. My guide whooped and cheered the horses on as they dodged the wayward walker or stationary obstacle. Each horse snorted with such ferocity and moved with such deft athleticism, that I couldn't help but feel that they must have been both delighted and proud in themselves.

How they knew the path without the driver's use of reins or a whip baffled me. Were they in fact like the cat and somehow privy to the wants and whims of human emotion? Or rather, I wondered to myself, was coercion and control simply not possible in this world? Freedom of all spirits seemed the primary directive of those around me.

We bounded back towards the park and down along its side. With a quick left turn, we clipped the bottom and galloped around the roundabout. A screech and a hard jolt brought us to a sudden stop. I caught my chest with my hand just in time to feel the quick thumping of my very-much-alive beating heart. My legs buckled underneath me as I jumped from the carriage.

"Bon voyage," my guide called out with a wave and a jump to the ground.

The driver tipped his hat, the horses neighed, and the carriage riders waved goodbye then they were off to their next destination, wherever that may be. I noticed that this part of town seemed to be cultivated in an attempt to create some semblance of order. Here, the trash had been cleaned and transformed. For example, a forest had been created along the sidewalks to give it an appearance of not just a tree lined street, but more of a makeshift jungle resplendent with flora and fauna. Everywhere I looked, something sparkled in the ghostly moonlight.

Couples in fine dress walked arm in arm around us. I use the term "fine dress" loosely, for they were outfits made from the odd bits of garbage and trash. Delicate flowers had been carved from used plastic bottles and long trains were adorned with intricate designs made from the pages of discarded books. Tattered top hats were made fine again with the addition of loose and mismatched buttons, glossy magazine decoupage, and even the occasional found feather or two.

From a world of dirt and grime, we had stepped into a world of elegance and order. I found myself much more at peace in this place, perhaps because it reminded more of my own home. I was a tidy person by nature. Even as a child I would vacuum my room daily. Tidiness and order were my two leading tenants of life. Here was where I belonged.

"This is lovely," I said as I touched the delicate leaf of a tree, which was made from an old receipt for a bottle of toilet cleaner.

"Is it?" My guide asked as he looked around. "I don't see it as anything more than anything else we've seen. This is just different in its transformation. Me? I prefer the chaos. This is for you."

"Thank you for that."

"I also need a drink and they have the best martinis."

"Here!" He swung open a hefty glass door (which had been meticulously polished). "After you."

We arrived at a neat lobby made of a composite of marble and metal. All manner of coats and hats were piled into an overflowing coat check just to the left of us. A woman with a hole in her head sat behind the counter casually reading a paperback book that looked as if it were missing several of its pages along with the back cover. She looked up a bit hopeful that we had a coat to check, but upon seeing we didn't, she simply returned to her reading. I found it interesting that she didn't at all seem bored, or resentful, of the tediousness. Instead, she seemed to treat the work as casually as if she had been at home on a Sunday afternoon reading a book in the sunlight.

I realized that we weren't in the restaurant itself, but rather a formal greeting area for to the restaurant. The building was a composite of uses, representing all that it had been in its previous lives. This was only a small part of it. To arrive there, I guessed that we were meant to ascend.

"About that," my guide said as we walked back to an enclave, which I assumed housed an elevator. "The elevator hasn't been retired yet," he said as he opened what would have been the elevator door. "They've done what they could, but it's a bit of a walk-up situation."

In the elevator shaft, the denizens had concocted a winding and haphazard staircase made of discarded and disused artifacts. A step here was comprised of office papers and another from pressed bricks of used coffee grinds. Everything else was stacked in between: steel rods, carriage wheels, tire irons, and mounds and mounds of packing peanuts. The crunching and crashing above us let us know that we were not the only ones in use of the strange staircase.

My guide happily began to climb. I was much more hesitant. A quick look up revealed no end in sight. I took a step slowly, testing the foundation to see if it would hold. Each step felt like a step of faith. There was no sound reason to believe a construction like this one would hold. Then again, this was not the world of logic and sense I knew.

As I climbed a slow pace up the constructed staircase, I wondered about faith and blindness. Was there something I myself was blind in all of this? Not just with this journey, but with the impetus that started it all: my struggle to bring life into the world. My own childhood had been devoid of love and tenderness. My parents and I viewed it as a kind of obligational contract. You: child. Us: parents. We: family. Nothing specifically tragic occurred, but it still made me feel incapable of welcoming a child into my life.

Testing my theory of faith, I tried to step confidently and erase the years of worry, stress, and strain. Unbuilding was hard work. I let the mess of it all just be, telling myself there was nothing to fix and nothing to tidy. What was, just was. If I could let go, for a moment then perhaps I could free myself from the shackles I had made.

Lost in my thoughts, I accidentally stepped on a crushed can of beans. The sticky sloppy mess stuck to the bottom of my shoe. When I went to wipe it off, I figured why bother? Something about the dirtiness of it, even if it was on the bottom of my shoe, made me feel like I fit in somehow. So much so that I—ready to dirty myself some more—stepped right in the middle of a puddle of unknown substance.

"Hey, watch it!" The puddle shouted back at my foot. An arm raised itself out of the trash and a foot followed.

"I am so sorry," I said backing away with a little apologetic bow as if that could help.

"Hey, Earl!" My guide said as he came bounding down the stairs. "Someone bothering you?"

"This idiot here stepped right on me!" The puddle shouted in response. "And on purpose too!"

"I'm sorry about that, buddy. " My guide gave me a tsk-tsk before saying, "This one's new around here. How about I bring you a drink on the way back?"

"Why bother?" Earl the puddle replied. "I ain't got a stomach!"

They both laughed as I stood there silently wiping Earl off my shoe. I had never accidentally stepped on someone in an attempt to dirty my shoes with their liquefied innards. Was there a proper decorum for these things?

"But bring some of that whiskey sauce if you think of it," said Earl the puddle with an emphatic wave of his two remaining limbs.

"You got it!" My guide said as he took my arm. "Bad accident," he said with a hushed whisper. "The explosion took most, well, all of his body, but even that couldn't stop him from making bad jokes," he said as we climbed up the final set of stairs.

"Here we are," my guide said as he craned open the elevator shaft's door.

The plainness of the elevator shaft was a fool's trick compared to the grandeur of the restaurant. Despite the derelict nature of the contents they were given, the denizens had crafted and shaped each scrounged item to convey a collected elegance. There was no shiny thing there, but together they all dazzled. Perhaps the most stunning of all, were the full panel windows that had been carved out along the far end of the restaurant. The result was a view of the city in all its dilapidated splendor.

Soft trembling light illuminated the room. Upon closer inspection, I saw that it was the light of a thousand fireflies all perched in the broken chandeliers. They were all dressed with the tiniest of top hats and appeared to be hobnobbing with a rather jovial spirit. There were little pools in the center of the chandelier that held a firefly punch that each bug would occasionally sip with a rather dignified dip.

In the center sat a grand piano with a rather amused looking pianist trilling a soft and light tune from the tips of his fingers. He had taken careful attention to wrapping his broken fingers with pieces of worn tape and had fixed the missing piano keys with sturdy combs and pieces of porcelain plates.

We settled into two seats at the bar, which was made out of a smooth marble with a burnt patch at the end from some past fire. The burn marks had been enhanced with artistic details and flourishes that made it appear as if the smoke could rise up out of the stone. Patrons sat on either side of us, speaking in hushed but pleasant tones. A bartender approached us with a businesslike manner.

"Huh-lo, martinis?" He asked.

"One for me and one for my friend," my guide replied. "Better make that two for me," he cupped his hand and motioned at me, "slow drinker this one."

The woman next to me carried on a long conversation with a man, who casually took off his head and placed it on the bar. She continued to orient her conversation to the head, which replied with just as much intensity. The body scratched at some itch in the center of his neck before returning the head atop the body once more.

"So," I said. "Is this the big revelation yet?"

"Do you feel revealed?" He asked with just a hint of exhaustion to his tone.

I felt like a child in the moment: stupid from not knowing the rules of the world around me and somewhat clumsy in my manner. Something had shifted. That much I could sense. My companion had moved his attention elsewhere while I was left alone in his company. *What had I done wrong?* I wondered.

"Drinks, se-rz," our bartender returned with a tight movement as he placed the drink in front of us with a curt manner.

"All business this one." I said as a kind of a lame joke.

"Don't even talk to me about *business*," he said with a lean onto the bar. "The latest news from down below is that the market is booming—booming! Just when I get out of it all."

We answered simultaneously: "What market?"/ "Isn't that the way it goes?"

72

"You're telling *me*!" He scoffed as he walked away, his head still shaking.

"What was that about?" I asked.

"He's new around here," he said with a long drink. "Still a little caught up in everything. Can't really blame him though. I think he was the wealthiest person in the city by the time he died."

"Now he works as a bartender?" I asked a bit too disdainful.

"Told you," He said, "things don't work like that down here."

"I don't follow."

"Look, for most of this guy's life he's had people waiting on him, which means he hasn't experienced it the other way around." He swiveled out to the room. "Most of the servers and cooks here were some of the most powerful and wealthiest people in their time. Now? They've chosen to experience serving and giving. Like I told you, it's all about balance."

"Who would want to work in death?"

"It's not about that!" He slammed down his drink on the bar. "Life and death are about creating for creation's sake, you idiot!"

"Yes, yes, yes." I cowered from his sudden anger. "I understand," I said cooing and trying to quell his anger.

"I don't think you do." He drained his drink in an angry gulp before leaving.

I was alone.

"Lovers' quarrel?" The bartender asked as he scooped up the empty glass.

"What? No." I answered. "Were you really . . ." I shook my head, "I'm not sure how to ask this?"

"You mean was I extraordinarily wealthy when I died?" He asked with a bit of a wink. "I was!"

"Then why do this?"

"Why do anything?" He answered. "Look, life is about choice. So why shouldn't death be the same thing?"

73

"I don't understand." I said. "I'm beginning to think I don't understand anything about anything."

"Then you're starting to get it!" My headless bar companion said as he pulled off his head and craned it closer to my conversation.

"That's exactly right." The bartender said . "You're getting too caught up in the semantics of it all."

"It's nothing to lose your head over!" Said the head.

"Look around you," the woman next to me said with a swift swizzle in her chair. A rather large hole in her chest oozed a little. "We could all chose to wallow and weep for the lives we had, the situations we find ourselves," she said with a point to her chest, "and the fact that we are quite literally living in garbage. Do you see anyone here doing that?"

"I haven't seen a sad face since I got here," I replied.

"And why do you think that is?" She asked me.

I sat in silence for a moment, thinking it over to myself. Why had I, alone, continued to make myself a caricature of moroseness in the world of the dead? I wondered how long I had been doing that in life.

"It's a choice," I said. "Balance," I muttered to myself.

"Everything is a choice," she said.

"Even in death," I said with a smile.

"And how did you die?" The head asked as it looked me over a few times. "You seem in surprisingly good shape for a dead guy!"

"I should probably catch up with my . . . friend," I said. Instinct told me that my being alive might cause some kind of unwanted reverberation. Not wanting to displace the cosmic harmony, I figured it would be best to stay silent on my condition.

"He's around," the bartender said. "You can probably catch him coming up on the parade."

"The parade?" I started to ask and decided against it. "Thanks," I said addressing my bar companions, "I needed that."

"Cheers!" They replied as they turned back once more to themselves.

I downed the rest of my martini in one fell swoop, which instantly made me almost faint and throw up simultaneously. Images flooded into my mind of martinis past: piano music, a beach, olives, and the feeling of a hand holding mine. I wasn't sure I would ever get used to it, but maybe it would make more sense when I was dead. The thought cheered me and I smiled. With one last look around and a swipe of a boat of whiskey sauce off a tray, I was gone.

"Hey, Earl," I said as I bounded down the stairs. "Your sauce!"

"Pour it on me!" He said with his arm and leg in the air.

I poured with gusto, letting the contents splash and spill. Casting the dish aside, I bounded down the grand makeshift staircase, past the coat check, and out the glass doors. I stood against the side, letting people pass me by as I wondered at my next move. Moments later, sounds of rooting and cheering rippled through the air.

Great big balloons of clowns, cats, and cartoonish creatures bobbed up and down in the ghostly air. Bands with tattered uniforms and banged up instruments followed. Make shift floats rolled along the bumpy road. Groups of people danced and cheered from atop the floats. This was, I gathered, a remnant of the Thanksgiving parades of the past, moving in reverse in this upside-down world. Just when I had thought of jumping aboard and catching a ride uptown, I saw my guide dancing with a woman on board a float. I let out a long whistle and rushed up to the float through the crowds that gathered with a casual but polite phrase ("pardon me," "excuse me," and "you dropped your hand").

Still unaware of my presence, my guide continued to dance. I let out another long whistle as I hoisted myself onto the float. A rather bemused individual with half of their body crushed reached out to lift me up onto the float with a muffled, "weeelll hellooo there!"

"Thanks!" I replied with a cheerful slap on his still intact shoulder. With a smile and a shimmy, he found himself a dance partner and continued in the tribulations.

With a beat in my step, I danced my way over to my guide. With a casual, "May I cut in?" I made my presence known.

"You!" He said as his partner danced away to another. "What are YOU doing here?" He puzzled it over with a tilt and scratch of his head, "I could have sworn I dropped you off ages ago," he muttered to himself.

"You didn't," I laughed, "but I think it's time I go back." I shrugged casually. "I have some living to do, while I got it."

"Ha!" He said with a guffaw and a slap on my back. "Now that's the spirit!"

I watched the city of the dead as we rolled back uptown. The chaos I had seen was still present and ever flowing. Now, I saw it for its individual details and the never-ending stories upon stories each thing held. Something in that, of not being discarded and forgotten, rang a clear bell of hope for me. For nothing was ever really in vain. No good deed ever really forgotten. The malaise of the day to day and the fear of a meaningless life were part of something grander. There was a grand mechanism at work, but perhaps it wasn't the great shiny and distant thing I had imagined.

Music filled the air and I danced along with it. Crowds gathered on either side of the float calling out to us with playful hoots and jubilant cheers. The balloons bobbed in step merrily. Sadness filled me at the thought of leaving, but my life was with the living. With a nod to my guide, we hopped off the float into a rather plushy bush by the park's entrance.

"Thank you," I said as we walked up the hill, "for making me *balanced* again."

"Balance," he said with a thoughtful nod. "Hey," he said with a snap of his fingers as if he remembered something suddenly. "Still thinking of having that baby?"

"We'll see," I said.

"Good," he said with a gentle mutter, "good, good."

Spirits of the earth, creatures of the ground, and humans of long, long past roamed all around us. I could feel now, the kind of pull that the gate in the rock had for me.

Where I had been eager to run away, I now felt drawn to return.

We entered back to the world of the living with no ceremony. I wondered if one was ever even needed anyway. No longer was I a child in need of guidance. The lights of the park were lit amongst a twilight sky. The moon lifted low in the horizon. Its light was full, shining down upon a bright and tidy cityscape. Night was still young. I had not missed too much time. No one would be worried, of that much I was certain.

"This is goodbye?" I said as we approached the bench where I had first met my guide.

"For you," he said as he reached behind the bench and pulled out an unopened iced tea in a brown bag. "For me, I drink and I wait, and I wait and I drink." He opened the can and leaned back a bit.

I watched as he disappeared into the backdrop of the park. He was there, but less and less so with each passing moment. Sounds of the city slowly returned to me: a siren rang, car horns honked in sharp bursts, and conversations of people passing by bubbled around me. I was home and the moon shined down upon me.

Rosalie, Oh Rosalie

Long awaited spring was in the air and every New York was out and about as if it could be the last. Rosalie couldn't stand all the busyness. Just wait until July, she thought, when these urbanites have gotten their fill of the heat and stowed themselves away in their tiny apartments to sit out the rest of the warm season with the artificial cool of window air conditioners.

Everything smelled wet and new. Buds had only just begun to form on the spindly branches and leaves were soon to follow. Rosalie adored the brightness of the fresh green leaves as they first unfolded and then settled into darker shades by summer's end. The newness of the season felt refreshing after the darkness and emptiness of winter. Spring was the season of reincarnation. The earth itself reawakened and became something different than it had been the year the before. Branches were a little taller. The grass had moved a little to the left. New flowers blossomed.

Rosalie wondered what the trees would say if they could talk. Would they bend low to admonish dogs for peeing on their roots? As she entered the park, Rosalie tuned into the arboreal vibrations around her. She tried her best to tap into the communications of the flora and fauna that rustled at her feet. Rosalie thought about the trees and wondered what messages they sent to the deaf ears of the casual strollers with their headsets plugged in and noses buried in the bright screens. She looked at the textured trunks, as if looking for messages to appear in the patterns of the wood, the crevices of the bark, or the knobs of the limbs. If they had responded to her callings, then she had not heard.

The winding trails of the park were an exercise in constant movement. She could almost forget she was in a city at all, until the occasional skyscraper poked out from over the treetops. Rosalie often came here for the pure joy of losing herself amongst the wandering paths and tall trees. She could escape from the pressure of the city to be always going somewhere, always doing something, or always seeing someone. There was no end game inside the whimsical twisting paths. Here diversions were rewarded with pleasant discoveries: a secret space in the rock, a hidden overlook, or a quiet spring.

Every breath and beat within herself felt reverberated against the aliveness of the trees in a way the city skyscrapers never could satisfy. In the dense thicket of buildings, the city merely felt reflected upon itself—an endless cycle feeding into the human whims and emotions around it. Inside the heart of Central Park, the plants and trees added a second element to the rush and hum of human vibrations. The two were in a beautiful dance with one another, unfolding and creating something new between them. Rosalie had always felt that the park represented the very best of the natural and human world combined. To her, it was the Garden of Eden set amongst the harsh and brutal wilderness of the city.

Sweat trickled down her brow in a way she had not felt in months and her heart beat wildly. Couples bathed in the freshness of spring. Children chased balls around the patches of newly grown grass. Dogs frolicked on short leashes. Groups of people enjoyed long moments of nothing on picnic blankets.

By the time she met Christian at the little pond with the boats, or rather the café by the pond that served wine and beer, Rosalie felt alive. Christian had perched himself at the very edge of the courtyard. Already, tables were filling up around him. He had a way of lounging coolly in a crowd: head cocked just a little to watch whatever interesting thing that was happening, one hand that never left his drink, his other arm casually leaning on something, and legs crossed for the sole purpose of bringing whatever patterned socks he had chosen to the attention of those around him. Christian had amassed a collection of empty beers on the table. Rosalie wondered what fresh hangover he was nursing today.

"I tried to save this for you." He said as she sat down across from him.

"Well, I can finish it for you," she said as she pulled his drink away from him. He looked somewhat aghast at her

80

boldness, which delighted her all the more. "You owe me that much for carting this picnic basket all across Manhattan."

"Look at you," He said with a smile as he gathered the picnic basket and offered his arm.

"That smile of yours could let you get away with anything." She reached for him and met him with a kiss.

"What makes you think it hasn't?" Christian laughed as he lifted her hand to kiss the back of it. It was one of the purest things Rosalie had ever seen him do. Christian never stood still, but here he was looking back at her with an expression of joy for the sake of the moment.

As they walked, Rosalie rested her head against his shoulder. She could feel love here. She was sure of it. The gesture was fleeting as Christian tripped over an unseen root and knocked into her head.

"That's not very practical," he growled.

"How about here?" She waved away his outburst and pointed ahead.

"Here is better."

"Whichever one is fine." She knew it was easier to agree with him than not.

With a flourish, he kissed her head. She interpreted it as a kind of apology, which was the best she would ever get from him. In the year she had been dating him, Christian never said what he meant or meant what he said. Rosalie told herself that was what kept him intriguing. He turned everything into a game, except that Christian's game was much like playing croquet with the Red Queen where the rules were bent to someone else's favor.

"Allow me." Christian spread the picnic blanket per his usual aplomb. He unpacked the basket, detailing each item as if he had picked them out himself. "And of course," he said as he reached for the bottle of rosé, "the most important part of any picnic." With a pop and a pour, the two of them laid back against the grass.

Rosalie felt herself getting lost in their casual conversation. She wanted to slip under Christian's words to unravel their meaning. The longing to know him poured forth from herself so strongly that it made her catch her breath. She wanted to feel Christian's skin against hers and uncover the purest parts of himself, but there was always something heavy and foggy between them.

Their conversations lulled and Rosalie pulled out a book she had recently purchased on the language of plants, which had become a kind of obsession for her. The way plants communicated with one another made her envious of their life. In vast underground systems, each tree was connected to the other. The way trees shared nutrients with one another, freely and without shame or guilt, was something that felt so lost to her. Theirs was pure connection.

"Darling, *why* are you doing this to yourself?"

Rosalie looked up from the passage she had been reading. Beside her, Christian laid on his side propped up on one elbow with his legs extended in his typical casual and careless manner. He felt neglected and was a bit annoyed, both of which he wanted her to know.

"You're never going to find the answers in there," Christian continued, "Instead, come and join me here. It's a beautiful day, we have a lovely picnic, and vino a la rosé," he took a long drink. "Don't be so serious. Carpe diem, mon amor."

"Diem carpe'd." She put down her book and picked up her drink once more.

"I decree today a day of passion and pleasure," he smiled and sat up to kiss her on the mouth. "All must obey the great god of Christian Lauder," he said as he lifted his cup into the air.

She laughed and smacked his arm. "You are insufferable. Did they teach you to be so obnoxious or were you just born that way?"

"Both, I think," he said as he ripped a piece of baguette and stuffed it into his mouth. "Don't act as if you aren't charmed. I know that sweet little squeal of yours," he said as he squeezed her knee (and she did indeed squeal despite herself). "New York City has finally agreed to be pleasant and

82

spring is here. Let's pretend that nothing else matters for one afternoon."

Christian plucked a nearby bloom and handed it to her. Rosalie held the flower in her hand. It almost seemed to curl around her palm, as if looking for a place to set down new roots. Rosalie had never noticed before how much plants moved. The pulsing of her beating heart matched the pumping life force that was now slowly drawing out of the flower. She could almost cry.

"Well, don't look so dreadful," Christian chided, clearly annoyed that his present was not well received.

"Not the usual response?" Rosalie said, as she pushed the flower behind her left ear and forced a smile. Rosalie felt as if the flower bent down to whisper something in her ear. She could feel it coaxing her and reassuring her, even in its moments of dying.

"That's better," Christian replied as he poured her more wine.

She pushed the stirrings within her aside, and turned her attention back to Christian. If you can't beat him, she thought, might as well join him. Rosalie gave in and drank deep. The sun shined down on her skin, hungry for its rays.

After a sweet afternoon with each other, the two of them watched the sunset from an outdoor table near the park—on the East Side of course. Rosalie found it somewhat charming that Christian referred to the restaurant as a café. True, she he had reasoned, the outdoor seating was more relaxed than the white tablecloth interior, but there was no getting over the expensive bottles of wine and overpriced dishes that poured out from within the polished interiors of old oak.

Rosalie watched early blossoms drift in the breeze. The sun was setting just early enough to remind everyone that winter's dark clutches were still around them in the elongated nights. Today's warmth was one small victory. Rosalie breathed in the evening air as if she could ingest the smell of summer returning.

"Are you even listening?" Christian asked, taking another oyster from the broad silver plate perched atop a pile of ice.

He had been going on about some ordeal pertaining to the liquor lockers at the most recent social club he had joined somewhere or another. And no, she had not been listening.

"It sounds like the frustrations of the upper crust have struck again," she gave him a wink, "and—to no one's surprise—you're the target."

"You could try to not be so condescending," he responded grumpily as he poured more wine for himself.

"I'm sorry," she leaned forward and motioned for him to pour some for her as well. Nothing could cheer up Christian more than the embodiment of a drinking buddy for the evening. It was a trait Rosalie knew he liked about her.

"I'm glad it's spring again," she tapped her glass against his. The trees across the way seemed to shake in agreement with her.

***

That night Rosalie dreamt . . . she was in her office. Water dripped from the panel above her. The water came on slow, drop by drop at first, until it rippled down with the steady stream of a kitchen sink and burst through the ceiling with the intensity of a fire hydrant. All the while, she kept working. Water lifted her chair, but she kept her balance still typing away and sending emails. Sparks flew as the wiring in the computer shorted out and the power died. Still, she kept typing. Pens and pencils floated in ink-stained water.

Rosalie's fingers kept typing at a phantom key board, as if she were still attached to her desk. Water poured over the sides of the cubicles and pressed against the windows of the building. The glass creaked. Like a dam releasing, the window burst open and water poured down the sides of the building. Everything else followed.

She floated on a river filled with office supplies down through the streets of midtown Manhattan. Street signs, food

84

carts, and bystanders both tourists and business alike were swept away by the growing force of the river. Like some wild beast acting on its own accord, the river rolled through corridors made by skyscrapers. The sound of the river's wild roaring filled the city.

When the river arrived at the bottom of Central Park it slowed into a calm hum. Previous signs of humanity disappeared and all that was left were the trees. Rosalie laid back in the clear cool water and let herself float on through the leafy treetops with a full moon shining above her.

***

Rotten sugary sweet breath puffed from her mouth. The sourness of her exhales felt wrong against the crisp air. Bright morning sun shone down through the leaves, making everything seem brighter and more vibrant. All it did was make Rosalie's headache worsen. Early morning joggers zoomed past her. Where she had felt so in synch with her surroundings just the day before, now she felt out of place, conspicuous, and exposed. Monday mornings could be a cruel push into the realities of her life she avoided so carefully on the weekends.

As she walked through the park, she found herself getting annoyed at how contrived the park was in its design. Even the just so placement of the trees and plants bothered her. Why did something have to grow *there* when perhaps it wanted to be *here*? Rosalie found it somewhat frustrating that people were shaping their environs to their wills and wants, which were forever changing anyway.

Her feet fell in time with the pounding of her heart. Rosalie thought she might die of a heart attack it was beating so hard—not totally unheard of for someone her age. Every decision she had made the previous day felt foolish in retrospect. The picnic basket hung limp and light beside her.

This morning her head throbbed in and out of varying intensities. A large part of Christian's appeal was that nothing was ever dull, boring, or relatively normal. Every night was a party. Every moment was an opportunity for fun . He would pull her into designer stores on whims just to have her try on whatever the mannequin had been wearing. If a weekend seemed particularly dull, he would whisk her off to spontaneous getaways at his family's house upstate, their house in the Hamptons, or even once, to the family compound in Bermuda. As exciting as all that was, Rosalie could only take Christian in small doses.

Rosalie wound her way through the thickets of trees. Today, the stones were speaking to her. The thudding of her heart spoke to their sturdiness and grounding. Stones spoke slowly. Their language was one of eons and epochs instead of seconds and minutes. They had a way of bringing perspective to the mercurial. *Slow down*, they whispered. *Don't rush. Be still.*

There was no time for that today. The sun was still fresh in the sky, but she was already late. Rosalie was barely holding onto her job by a thread. Ducking and covering could only last for so long. Showing up late, disheveled, and obviously hungover were not viable options. Half the time it didn't stop her. Thinking about the day ahead made her groan and rub her temples.

Rosalie let her feet beat upon the earth. The rumblings and stirrings in her stomach began to crawl upwards in a fiery fashion. With a lurch and growl, Rosalie lunged into the nearest bushes. The evening's contents poured out with a primal and guttural sound. Sweat beaded upon her skin and she shook from the force of it. Her heart thudded in her chest as she shakily walked onward.

"Morning," she mumbled to her doorman as she entered her building. The lobby was as clean and bright as ever. Rosalie could barely afford the rent for her small studio. Wasn't that the price of being in the city? She always asked herself. Almost as if she were reminding herself of her own dreams, which felt ever more distant with each passing day.

When she got to her apartment, she peeled off her clothes immediately and went for the shower. She let the cool water run over her body. Dirt and grime flowed off of her in

86

tiny streams. Rosalie imagined these bits of herself flowing down and through the pipes making their way towards the rivers and oceans. Rosalie felt almost envious that they could escape, but was happy that at least a part of her was free.

When she returned to the streets once more, the city hummed and buzzed with life. This time, the joggers zooming past were replaced with men in smart suits and women in sensible flats pushing forward en masse to and from the trains. The mad dash of rush hour always threw Rosalie in a bit of panic. People were so certain of where they were going that it made Rosalie feel unnerved, because she was never certain.

Smashed in together, strangers touched and bumped each other with silent annoyance. Commuters shuffled in and out of the stale train cars. Rosalie hated the way people were pushed and forced together in the tense crowded spaces like cattle for the slaughter. Nothing made her feel so much a part of the machine than the morning commute. There they all were, like a mass sacrifice, being pulled towards the gods of commerce and economy.

From the first moment off the train and onto the platform, midtown was an explosion of human energy. Everywhere there were people squeezing in through crowds, pulling along suitcases, and operating their bodies much like the cars on the streets beside them. People pushed past in heavy crowds that threatened to sweep Rosalie away in one strong current.

Rosalie shut her eyes for a second and imagined everyone turned into trees. Midtown ceased to be a place of noise and pollution, and in an instant, transformed into a serene grotto. Sidewalks were filled with trees. Branches intertwined and reached upward to the sun as if in praise of its light.

"You planning on walking today?" A man grumbled under his breath at Rosalie.

In that instant, the dream was shattered, and the city returned to itself as it was. She was amongst the temples to corporations and consumers once more. If she didn't come with a smile and the gift of herself as sacrifice, they could smell her out in an instant. Rosalie knew her life and livelihood depended on it, but she had reached a point where she could no longer fake it like she once could. There was no end to the tedious and pointless tasks of promulgating a portfolio of goods that brought no one lasting happiness for all their promises. Everything was being rotated in and out in an endless and mind-numbing loop. What kind of forced enthusiasm could be upheld in the madness of the city, she wondered as she swiped her key card into the lobby of the office building.

Her family had inculcated her at an early age about the importance of college and getting a "real job." To them, the only acceptable forms of living were ones that consisted of being within a cubicle, or perhaps one day, a corner office. Her parents had translated corporate success into a resume ready relationship, which seemed obligatory—if not annoyingly inconvenient. They liked each other enough, and perhaps, they really even did love one another in their strange way. Theirs was the kind of steady relationship Rosalie could depend upon for a stable upbringing. To Rosalie, however, it looked miserable.

That's why she fell in love with Christian, she told herself. He was anything but tamed. Each whim and fancy were his in the instant. Everything was pleasure. Rosalie felt at her throbbing temple to remind herself that even that was a gilded cage.

She found herself lost somewhere between her parents and Christian. If she was being honest with herself, Rosalie wasn't achieving much in this non-space. Rosalie often felt adrift in the mass tides of people in Manhattan, wondering how and where to turn but unable to row. Life felt easier floating along. Clarity was never a strong suit of hers, especially when the whole world seemed to be rowing away from her. There was no endgame to her desires. She wondered if that was a new path forged on the road to enlightenment: the subtle art of not-giving-a-damn. Somehow it didn't feel like nirvana.

Rosalie laid her head onto the cool of the desk. Nonstop air conditioning turned the plastic into a perpetual cold pack. A bout of nausea washed through her and she only just made it into the trash can beneath her desk (silently of course). She fought every urge she had to curl up under the desk like a fox in its den in the woods, but there was work to be done.

There were emails to check, meeting requests to accept, and work flows to review. Her inbox was a never-ending stream of ego trips and vitriol. People made such a fuss over such unimportant things. The whole system was inherently fleeting. The agency she worked for would fold. The brands they worked with would fold. The world itself would end. And still, people buzzed around as if the work they were doing would last forever.

Rosalie opened her drawer to the stash of anti-nausea and pain relievers she had stashed away for moments just like this one, which were happening more and more frequently. Her life had gotten to a point where it was literally making her sick. She took the medicines dry, making a rather ridiculous seagull motion as she tilted her head back to let the pills slide down her throat via gravity. There were some moments she was grateful for the walls.

"Roh-sie, Rosie, Roh-sie . . . how was your weekend? Aren't you *so* ready to get out of this place already?" A thin attractive blonde sidled over to Rosie's desk and sat on the edge with an oversized mug in her hands.

"Lucy, could you take it down a notch—or five?" Rosalie rubbed at her temples.

Lucy laughed. "How is that gorgeous rich boyfriend of yours?"

"Still good, still gorgeous, still cheap as ever."

"If I don't steal him away from you someday . . ."

"Nice try, but his father's fourth wife cured him of his interest in blondes."

"*Anyway*," Lucy waved away the dig, "Roger wants you in his office *stat*."

"What now?"

Lucy shrugged before helping herself to the jar of candy Rosalie had received last year at a conference. Rosalie would have forgotten entirely about it were it not for the jar. Good marketing, she thought.

"Probably wants to talk about the Southeast sales division," Lucy said as she uncurled the wrapper and popped the piece of chocolate into her mouth. "After that dreadful—bleh, how old is this?" She spit it out and balled it up into the wrapper before tossing it into Rosalie's trash can. "After that dreadful sales report this morning—which I covered for you *again* by the way and you're welcome—he probably wants to talk to you mano a mano."

"Got any advice for the lion's den?" Rosalie replied as she fished for a pen in her drawer.

"No clue, but he *does not* seem happy."

She popped another ibuprofen and left the sad little cubicle she inhabited seven hours out of the day. Rosalie often thought she was being housed in a modern-day livery stable and she was the horse in a stall made of pushpin ready walls with binders of presentations for fodder. Through the stillness of corporate dryness, she heard the single serving coffee machine sputtering to life, the printer humming away as it shot out spreadsheets, and keys clicking as they sent out email after email.

"Roger?" She knocked and turned the handle and peeked into the corner office, "Lucy said you were asking for me?"

Roger sat behind his large wooden desk, pounding down on the keys of his keyboard as if the sheer force of the pressure would increase sales. He always had a clean-cut suit and fresh cut hair. There was a kind of plastic quality to him, as if he opened a doll of himself in the morning, popping out of his box brand new for the day.

"Shut the door behind you, Rose." He stopped typing and turned to her with both elbows on the table. "There's no easy way to say this, so I'll just come out and say it. Our parent company has decided to turn over the business from our Southeastern division to another one of their agencies already running and operating in the area. They know the clients and the market better than we ever could. This isn't seen as a loss for the company, but it does mean that we'll have to make some cuts around here." He shook his head. "This is no easy decision, never is, but since the Southeastern division is under your supervision . . . well, we're going to have to let you go."

"What?"

"I know you've been here for," he looked at his computer screen, "three years, but don't worry. HR will review your severance package before you go." There was a knock. "Come in!" A large man in a security uniform opened the door.

"This can't be happening." Rosalie held her head in her hands. The nausea was taking hold of her body in sharp bursts.

Roger stood up and walked halfway around the desk, "I'm sorry to say it is. You understand, no hard feelings. Eh, Rose?" He extended his hand.

"All the feelings! *What the hell*, Roger?"

"Face it," he frowned. Sales were down in the division the moment you started here. I said, give her a chance she's bright, but if you brought half the energy to your job as you did in the beginning then we wouldn't be having this conversation." He motioned to the security guard who moved closer to Rosalie. "Face it, Rose, you don't want to be here. Move on. You're young. Find a job you actually like."

"Sure," Rosalie's face flushed with rage. She held up her hands as if surrendering, "I'll go." She made a motion to leave, but at the last second, she turned around and in one swift action cleared the contents from the mahogany surface of the desk. Down went the dual monitors, the keyboard, the shiny office supplies holder, the photos of Roger with his buddies in Cancun, the golf trophies, and the agency awards. As they all crashed to the floor the security guard pounced on Rosalie and pulled her arms behind her back. He marched her out of the office and into the hall.

She called over her shoulder, "And *for the record,* it's Roh-sa-lie!"

91

Behind the rows of printers and filing cabinets, Lucy mouthed, *what are you doing?* In response, Rosalie shot her a wide and wild grin. With a gentle but commanding shove, the security guard walked her out and down through the halls, past the glass doors, into the elevator, down through the marble lobby, and out onto the streets.

"Rosie!" Lucy came running out of the doors of building. She held a box in her arms rather awkwardly. "I'm so sorry," she puffed in between her shortened breaths. "I swear, I didn't know he would do that."

"It's okay, really," Rosalie said.

"Your things," Lucy offered the box to Rosalie. "I had enough sense to grab them before Roger had a chance to toss them into the trash." She laughed. "You really pissed him off, Rosie. The head of one of his golf trophies popped right off in the fall. Irony much?"

"Well," Rosalie laughed, "you better get back inside before they think you've defected."

"Best of luck, Rosalie." Lucy smiled and left.

Rosalie turned away from the building and looked up at the radiant sun overhead. She closed her eyes as she let the sunshine drip over her body. All around her were people hustling and bustling to and from locations. She stayed rooted as foot traffic flowed all around her.

"You going to stand there all day?" Someone said as they bumped into her.

After a while, Rosalie began to move. She had no map, no direction, and no cares. What was it like to be a part of the free world, she wanted to know; to wake up every day without a plan to *do* but a plan to *be*? Her life had been calculated and planned by her calculating and planning parents, but not once had she ever given it a thought about what she might want or what she might be instead.

She allowed herself to be moved by the ebb and flow of the crowds around her. Drifting like a fish in a stream, she let herself flow without any care or worry about the direction. When she found herself outside the golden doors of Grand

Central, she opened them and ventured inside its massive halls.

Rosalie had never been inside without a ticket. The station was always some in between place which was to be entered and exited quickly. Now, she let herself linger amongst the vaulted corridors. Intricate brass fixtures reflected a muted golden light on the cream-colored walls and floors. There was an elegance to it that felt old fashioned and out of place against the grey skyscrapers outside. Standing still, she looked upwards to trace the constellations on the turquois ceiling.

The crowds around her anticipated her stillness and inaction, moving past like trickling water. Rosalie could feel the mass web of humanity in motion. The stillness of the stars above felt like a reversal of fate. At night, it was the stars that moved across the sky as the people below stayed still to watch them. Here, the stars were still and the people pressed and pushed in motion below them. She was struck by the artificial beauty of it all. For while it was beautiful, it was all a well-crafted illusion at best.

Rosalie found herself suddenly hungry for something more real that she could put her hands on and touch and feel. Even in this grand hall, she felt stifled. Air was what she needed, and maybe Christian too. Rosalie launched herself out of the crowd and into a cab just outside. She couldn't go home. Going home would only break the illusion of manic joy and she wasn't ready to let the reality of the world come crashing down upon her. Moving forward felt right.

"Eighty-fifth and Fifth Avenue," she told the driver.

From the mirror above him, the driver eyed Rosalie's box in her hands. He gave a brief nod before proceeding down Madison Avenue. Shop after shop of expensive tastes rolled past her vision. For the first time all day, she felt panicked. The commercial world felt so far away from her. No longer was she a part of it and suddenly, nothing seemed worthwhile.

A wave of nausea passed through her once more. Rosalie rolled down the window and let her head rest in the cool breeze of the car's momentum down the avenue. The smells outside were harsh, unpleasant, and untraceable. They were the smells of the city rising up from the concrete and into the air all the way up to the highest skyscraper. She wondered if the only way to escape them would be to go downward and into the earth itself.

"Pull over here," Rosalie said as she pulled cash out from her purse. She had seen Christian on the sidewalk before the cab had even reached his building. "Keep the change," she called out as she slammed the door shut behind her.

Christian stood on the sidewalk just outside of a French restaurant where they often spent long afternoons sipping Sancerre and snacking on gougères. Today, he wore a classic straw hat with bright pink socks and a polo with khakis to match. He had perched himself against a tree on the sidewalk, which was a sure indication he was already drunk.

"Darling!" Christian startled as Rosalie walked up to him on the sidewalk. "What on earth are you doing *here*?"

He gave her long embrace. Rosalie inhaled the amber notes of his cologne that barely masked the smell of alcohol on his breath. Even his very skin smelled like bourbon setting in an old oak barrel.

"You wouldn't believe it," she said, "They let me go."
"Who did?"
"My job . . ." she said.
"I didn't realize you worked!" Christian said with a laugh. "No, I'm joking—don't look so upset. I do listen to you."
"Shall we grab a drink to celebrate my freedom?"
"Now? Oh, ah," he looked towards the restaurant door with a quick fidget.
"Are you with someone?"
"An old friend from school," he said.
"Well, there's more I wanted to tell you."
"There's more?"
"Now that I have the time, I was thinking we could maybe do some traveling," Rosalie said with her most flirtatious fingers-on-his-chest move that she knew drove him wild.

"Oh now, sweet Rose," he said with a nervous laugh and took her hand from his chest into his. "I don't think that my schedule—"

"What schedule?" She demanded, knowing that her voice had risen to the level of shrill but not really caring. When did Christian *ever* have a schedule? "We could go to Venice. Paris. Milan." Her voice rose. "You and me." The space between her words shortened. "We can wake up as late as we please. It will be lovely. We can go, we *should* go. What do you think?"

"Oh Rose," Christian said with a pained look. He put his hand on his head. "I just don't know about all that."

"What on earth do you mean?" Rosalie took a step backwards.

"That's just not me." Christian shrugged in a boyish manner.

"Gallivanting across the globe—that's not *you*?"

"Guilty of that, I suppose," he said with a charming smirk. "I'm just not a one-woman man. I thought you understood . . . we were just having a good time."

"You were having a good time," she said.

"Darling," he said as he reached for her arm. "Don't end it like this. Don't end it at all!"

She looked at his fingers curled around her bicep. There was a time when she would have felt electrified by his touch. Now, she felt nothing at all. "Goodbye, Christian." She hailed a cab without a second glance over her shoulder.

From behind her, she could hear the jingle of the restaurant's door followed by the cool clicking of stilettos against the sidewalk. Rosalie stepped towards a cab that was coming her way. "Who was that?" She heard a woman ask. As Rosalie stepped into the cab, she heard Christian reply, "Just an old friend, darling." With a swift pull, Rosalie closed the cab door.

"To the West Side," she said. "Seventy-fifth and Amsterdam."

Back to her apartment she went. For the first time that day, she lifted the lid off the printer paper box that Lucy had given her. The box contained a collection of Rosalie: a wide selection of over-the-counter medications and a single conference candy jar filled with rotten candy. Rosalie closed the lid. She had seen the contents of her life and it didn't look good.

She felt nauseated again and put her head in her hands. Everything had fallen apart and all it took was a single day. Rosalie had been playing her life by a set of rules someone else had made. Look what it had gotten her. Her stomach growled and grumbled so loudly that the driver looked back to ask her if she was alright.

"No lunch," she mumbled. No breakfast either, she thought.

As they drove through the 79th street transverse, Rosalie watched the newly budding trees. Everything was just as bright and sunny as it was yesterday, but under the lens of the cold context of the day, nothing seemed the same. Rosalie felt jealous of the plants and trees as they stood so carefree in the setting sun. They wanted for nothing. Their lives were as easy as that.

She arrived at her apartment with very little fanfare or grandeur, but Rosalie felt it to be momentous. There wasn't an exact thing that she could point to or any exact moment that felt particularly extraordinary, but she could feel the very ground beneath her feet shake. Above all, she was angry.

Rosalie fumed all the way up the elevator. All this time she had been living for other people's wills and wants without once questioning their intentions. She had no doubt that all her parents wanted from her was to use her to fulfill a better picture of themselves. Christian had wanted quick and ready companionship under the guise of romance. She was even fairly certain that her boss had hired her, knowing full well that she would fail, and that in firing her, he could boast streamlining which meant savings for the company, increased profits, and another shiny office for himself on a higher floor.

She had turned herself into an asset that people could measure and count against their own standing. Rosalie threw the box on the floor when she entered her apartment. Its once crisp cardboard sides had formed a pulpy and discolored exterior from Rosalie carrying it around all day. Like a mantra repeated during a meditation, anger moved through her body. Over and over, it churned.

Anger rolled and roared through her. Like a clawing thing that had been buried for too long, her rage had dug itself out of the grave she had built for it. Now it came tumbling out of her and she shook with the force. Rosalie screamed a deep primal sound and let it roar out of her.

Still, it wasn't enough. She wanted to rip apart everything, including herself. There was no room for logic or thought. Rosalie wanted to claw, rip, and tear through everything that had comprised her life. The box was the first to go as she ripped it apart and smashed the glass conference candy jar. She ripped apart the candy wrappers and crushed the medicines on the floor.

When that wasn't enough, she turned towards the kitchen. Down went the wine glasses as she held onto the stems and smashed their goblets on the countertop. Crash went the plates as she smashed them against the counter. Bowls, mugs, and even her spatulas, were no match against the raging storm. Spoiled leftovers from takeout containers splattered the walls as she ripped apart the containers and smashed the food in her hands.

After she had torn apart the kitchen, she pounced on the loveseat's cushions and tore the stuffing from their bodies. In a flurry of feathers, Rosalie ripped apart the pillows. She tore at the throws, shredded her books at their spines, and smashed the trinkets and bibelots on the shelves. Nothing was spared. She broke the heels off of her shoes, snapped purse straps in two, and tore at the shiny fabric of her cocktail dresses. As the sun continued to fall and the landscape grew darker, Rosalie ripped apart everything she owned. Her studio had turned into a mess of her own creation.

When at last she had destroyed her things, Rosalie ran towards the park. She ran because she didn't know what else to do. She ran because it was the only way she could escape. She ran because it made her feel free. Everything she had, every connection she had made, and every bit of the life she had created on someone else's orders, was gone.

Rosalie crashed through empty paths partially lit by old fashioned lamps. Her breath shortened as she climbed up the hills. Twigs cracked and broke under her feet. She dove through the paths, deeper and deeper into the trees. Her heart thudded in her chest like a captured songbird. She could feel it slamming against her ribcage to try and break free.

She fell down beside a little brook in the woods and shook with emotion. Finally, she let herself cry. She wept for everything that had gone wrong in her life, every moment when she could have made a choice, but didn't, and every moment when she could have made something matter, but couldn't. As she laid there in the dirt, she felt as if everything poured out of her with each teardrop and each sob. Rosalie emptied herself there by the creek. She let everything drain out of her and pour into the earth. When she felt as if she couldn't pour out anymore, Rosalie let the cool breeze of the night soothe and lull her.

All around her, the woods were awake. Bugs crawled on the mosses and stones. Streams bubbled and flowed. Raccoons rustled the fallen leaves in their search for food and late-night company. Spring moved around the trees and beckoned the warmth of summer to arrive and thaw out the earth after the long and hard winter. Like the seasons changing, an imperceptible shift occurred. There was a change, and yet, Rosalie found it hard to place just exactly when things had changed. Could it have been a degree warmer today than it was yesterday? Could the tips of flowers have grown an inch taller?

Finally, she heard the trees whispering, the water murmuring, and the long grasses chatter. The longing to be a part of them resonated so strongly within her that her heart felt like it was breaking. Her chest felt tangled and jumbled, as if something alive was squirming within it. When she looked down, Rosalie watched as tiny green roots began to grow from the center of her chest. They began as small luminescent hairs, barely visible at first. Rosalie breathed heavily and tilted her head up towards the canopy above her. Overhead, the full moon shifted from behind the clouds. Streams of light poked through the leaves and illuminated the forest with columns of light, shivering and shaking with an energetic fervor, as if they were willing a manifestation of a physical occurrence.

The spindly shapes of Rosalie's new roots grew thicker and stronger. She let them linger, feeling them curl around her fingers. Intuitively, she began to pull them gently towards the earth, where they buried themselves under the leaves and grasses. Upon contact, Rosalie felt something begin to flow within her. She was connected to the trees around her. Rosalie could feel them sending nutrients to her roots and communicating with her in a language that was so old, there were no words.

She tipped her heart towards the earth, letting the roots grow deeper. Her flesh began to harden and dip into a map of knots and divots. Rosalie listened to the language of the trees around her. Nothing was unknowable. She rested her ear to the earth to listen closer. Sounds of a thousand different voices resonated, but it wasn't just the trees. The streams and grasses, and even the Hudson and Harlem Rivers, were speaking in and through her.

Rosalie clawed her hands into the dried leaves and let her arms grow long into the earth. Her body was shifting and changing into a linear shape as her legs stiffened and lifted upwards towards the sky. Tiny pricks bristled against the thick skin of her legs as branches and leaves burst forth from within her. She could no longer remember her name, but it didn't matter. She had a new name, which was her true name, that the world had known her by for far longer than she could have ever known.

A Sturgeon's Tale

Leah sat very still at the windowsill watching the people below her. She felt like a cat in heat, itching to slink her way down the stairs and rub herself against a stranger, but she could not move a single inch. So, she watched their slick sweaty skins glittering in the gold summer sun from afar. They were a group of people united with one purpose, but little else: they came to brandish the flag of the sturgeon.

What had begun as a protest on behalf of the sturgeon, had transformed into a roving party that wound its way through the city. That summer, the sturgeon had traveled up and down the Hudson River, destroying everything in its path by the sheer enormity of its size. The city wanted it dead. Instead, for these people, the sturgeon was nature itself challenging the authority of man. The sturgeon had become a symbol of life itself, and its power was infectious.

Bright flashes of sunlight caught on the pots and pans people brought to drum upon when the mood suited them. Beads of fresh sweat flecked against their flesh like glitter. The mood to make music and dance struck them often and frequently, creating an uninterrupted stream of drumming and moving of hot and wet bodies. Bottles at varying capacities and emptiness swung wide with each turn and step of their made-up dance. Laughter and shouts bubbled up to Leah's window. She had heard them making music as they moved towards her, block by block, until at last they arrived. Leah watched her neighbors cautiously venture into the commotion with curiosity, only to be soon initiated with bottles swinging and kitchen pots beating wildly.

Leah was far too uncomfortable to even think of moving. A low but oppressive heat had risen in her apartment since early morning, culminating now in a crescendo of swelter that could only be combated by sitting very still. In that stillness, Leah could almost convince herself that she was relaxed lounging in the breeze that wafted into her apartment. Soft winds blew in the scent of the city, dripped in the cool promise of evening. There was always a tenderness to the shifting between the day and night. Leah could feel it now.

A collective cheer cried out below as the sun touched the earth and cast a perfect golden glow over the crowd. They were all radiant, soaked in the lusciousness of the light. The sun performed a jubilant finale as it cast its finest light of the day upon the earth and left with a triumphant bow.

Still beating their pots and pans, but now with less gusto, the crowd dispersed and night crept upon the city one star at a time. The heat of the day drained out of the windows of the apartment and Leah felt that she could at last move. She stretched out her legs and wrung out her neck and shoulders. With a final shake and shimmy of her body, she arose. The stillness of her days didn't bother her so much. Leah was more of a night person anyway.

A quick peek at the piles of take-out containers left in the fridge with only bits and small bites of food confirmed what she already knew: she was going out for dinner. Leah threw on a dress, a pair of comfortable shoes, brushed her hair, and was out the door. She never took too long to get ready. A life of natural beauty had that effect upon her, although Leah never thought of herself as beautiful. She thought of herself the way everyone thought of themselves, with little regard to her good qualities and perpetual worry and strain over her faults, of which she had many, or so she had been told.

Sirens echoed and search lights from above looked like dangerous angels descending onto earth. For three nights now, city officials had been looking for the giant sturgeon that had evaded everyone's grasp and continued to cause mayhem and destruction up and down the Hudson River. After months of complaints from fishermen, ferries, and casual boaters, a lawsuit threatened to take the city for all it was worth if they did not catch that fish.

The mayor, who was well aware of his declining popularity, set to the task of collecting all the appropriate personnel employed by the city. Quietly, but not unknown to his denizens, the mayor had suggested to big game hunting and fishing enthusiasts, hardened criminals, and those with a personal vendetta against the fish itself for damages wrought upon them by its hateful fin, that certain unnamed and unknown actions would be overlooked as long as they produced the body of the thing itself. Everyone knew the mayor wanted that fish's head upon his supper table.

They had set twenty-four-hour surveillances of the waterways with swaths of helicopters, cruisers, and coast guard boats that only seemed to grow in number each night. Radios, lights, sirens, and the incessant whirring of a chopper overhead polluted the otherwise calm and peaceful summer evenings. Leah grumbled and cursed at them each time a helicopter dipped overhead or a searchlight struck her in the eye. She was never one for politics, but about this she was certain: she was on the side of the poor damned sturgeon.

Bells from the nearby church rang out in between the screeches of the sirens, reminding everyone of a quieter time before the chaos in the sky. A soft echo of their song lingered and stilled the night air. A quick clip of a siren broke the enchantment and Leah was back to feeling itchy inside herself. She was restless too. Leah could barely focus her thoughts on any one single thing and instead indulged them in jumping from one strange fantasy to commonplace observations to theories of the human condition and back again.

Thick summer air pressed against her skin, forming heavy dewdrops as if she had just gotten out of the water. She was always wet in summer. Leah spent her mornings in the tub, cooling her body down from the inescapable heat of the sizzling city. Ice cold water ran hot down her head until she had sufficiently soaked for at least four hours in the water. Then, she would sit very still at the window until the sun retreated and the moon reigned in the sky.

Nights were when Leah got to the serious business of cooling down her body. She spent the time walking the long straight avenues of the city, feeling the whirl of the winds hurtling through the artificial tunnels the tall towers created along the wide avenues. She walked the long stretch of the Hudson River, slipping in and out of the shadows of the rocks along the water, letting the spray of the brackish water softly

103

tickle the tip of her tongue with its salty touch. She spent hours laying in the empty lawns of the parks, staring into the lights of the buildings like one might stare at stars.

Lately, Leah had been hotter than usual. Something inside of her had broken this summer. She could feel it. The thermostat of her emotional body was wildly amiss. During the past few days, she had spent a minimum of six hours in the ice-cold water of her tub with the lights turned off, so that the artificial night inside the windowless bathroom was drawn against the intolerable brightness of the day.

She couldn't place what it was that driven her to that state. The summation of her emotions was always too intense for her own body to hold. In fact, they had grown to such a boiling level in the dead heat of summer that all she could do was think of herself not as a body, but more as a container for the controlling and letting out of heat. She had become a kind of engine mechanism gauged to release heat and steam, while never managing to properly cool off but only ever achieving moments of equilibrium in such small and delicious quantities that they were moments always longed for, but rarely obtained.

At an earlier age, she had channeled these emotions through a moderately successful career as a visual artist selling her paintings, which heavily featured the Hudson River as a backdrop or even center piece, to her work. She couldn't even muster the energy to do that anymore. With a bit of luck here and there, and whatever financial resources were left from her earlier career, Leah had the rare freedom to do whatever she pleased: as long as what she pleased was of very little financial need. Luckily, Leah's habits had become so dismal and simultaneously spendthrift that if she were to maintain a life subsiding on long cold baths and a single meal a day that she had at least another twenty years of subsidized poverty ahead of her. Not that Leah minded her money or even cared how much was left in the coffers. It was all the same to her if she ran out tomorrow or in a hundred years.

The city sidewalks were alive with tables and chatter. Smells of onions and bread and smoke all filled the air with just as much life as the customers who consumed them. Ice cubes jingled against wet glasses as sudden and deep laughter punctured the air. As Leah walked closer to the Hudson River, she watched dogs on leashes pee with gleeful delight on roots of trees and the bottom of signs. Cars were in constant motion all around her. The sirens and flashing lights of the fish hunters were never too far out of sight or earshot.

Leah threw herself down at the little table amongst many more little tables that overlooked the river. Every night for the past three years, her evening began here at a small shabby restaurant with a clear view of the Hudson. Leah wasn't supposed to drink, but she did anyway.

"House red," she said to the waiter without so much as a hello, "and fries, the way I like them. The chefs know."

Her manner was off putting, which she knew but didn't care. Besides, everyone knew her well enough to not take it personally. The clientele were strictly locals with a penchant for saltiness. The occasional exhausted tourist or city wanderer might plop down for a beer before heading off to somewhere shinier with friendlier company. The food wasn't great and the drinks weren't anything too fancy, but it was a cheap place with a strong cooling wind and a wide view of the water, which suited her needs just fine.

She sat and watched the dark waters of the river. The silver light from the half-filled moon curiously peeked down on the world below it, casting light and shadow on the river. Here, she could let her mind unravel and reform. Leah thought of the waters as the very essence of the unknown. There was a comfort in the vastness of it. She sat like that, glass after glass, gazing at the water as if to divine some meaning from the moving darkness.

The incessant whirring of helicopters circled above her like giant insects, raining unwanted disturbances to those below them. Sirens and shouts filled the night sky like pollution from a thousand passing diesel trucks. Spotlights darted across the water, before concentrating on several large splashes. Shots fired out and Leah screamed.

The waters lifted in a moonlit arc with droplets forming an iridescent aura around the jumping fish, like stardust to a cosmic shower bursting from the heavens. In the center, Leah watched the sturgeon lift into the air with such athleticism and sportsmanship that a spectator might have thought the fish to be a competitor in a gymnastics match. The sturgeon's scales shimmered in the moonlight.

A thousand rounds of ammunition must have gone into its body in that moment. Shouts rang out and even with the trail of blood in the water, they continued to shoot for the sake of shooting. They wanted that thing dead. No one knew what was the splashing of the fish dying in the water or what was the splashing of the bullets entering it.

"Get'em good and dead!" The crowds shouted out as the rounds fired one after the other.

Leah couldn't take her eyes off of the scene in the water. The bullets tore into the waters as it ripped apart the delicate psyche of Leah. She couldn't stop her body from shaking and wine spilled all over the table. Her breath felt like it was out of her body.

She tried to still herself by gazing into a quieter patch of dark waters along the shoreline. A sudden stirring of the water and a quick flash of silver made her stop. If there was hope, she had to know.

Leah left the table and rushed to the water's edge. For the first time in a long time, she had no thoughts in her mind. She was pure body. Pure animal, she corrected herself as she ripped off her shoes to slip in and out of the rocks like she had a hundred times before.

She could smell the blood before she found the body of the sturgeon. In the shadows, the fish looked like another massive rock. When the clouds shifted and the moonlight poured down upon the water, the silver scales sparkled through the thick patches of muddy blood. The sturgeon manifested like a ghost. Its' massive body heaved for air as it lay in between the world of the water and the world of the land.

Cautiously, she crept toward the fish, who looked at her with its large round eyes. Chunks of its body were gone and blood mixed with the river mud to create a new kind of skin in its place. Leah let her hand rest on the small undamaged part of its body. The slippery flesh felt cool to her touch as she cooed and stroked the fish. In the sliver of nighttime light, she could see its flesh was marbled and mossy from years of being in the dark cool of the water. She tried to flush water into its lungs, but it was too late. With a final and bleak shudder, the fish stilled and stiffened and the waters around it calmed.

It was *wrong*, Leah thought as she began to shake again. She rested against the fish, letting her salty tears and thick mucus mix with the substance of the water, the blood, and the river mud. Leah looked up at the moon, as if somehow blaming it for what had happened when instead she knew it was the constant hunger and drive for vindication and violence that reigned in humanity that was to blame. Leah knew she was not separate from it and tried to take the violence that had been done to the fish upon herself. If she could take that away on behalf of humanity then maybe she could restore the life, the nature, of the fish.

Leah didn't notice the movement and sound escalating around her until someone shouted, "It's over here!" The spotlights and helicopters were all moving closer. She panicked. They could not have their prize, she decided. Leah looked at the massive size of the fish. There was room for her twice over. When they cut open their catch, she would be inside to ruin their spoils with the gruesomeness and strangeness of the human body inside of it. With the shouts and sirens drawing closer, Leah crawled into the mouth of the fish.

As she pressed her way into the fleshy mouth of the fish, Leah could fully taste the salt and decay of the river. She crept into the vast cavern of the fish's stomach still filled with water and the detritus of the river. There, she curled herself into a ball and waited for the end. In the acidic contents still

107

remaining in the fish's stomach, Leah could feel her skin and edges of herself dissolving.

The half-filled moon cast its light upon the sturgeon. Instead of becoming less and less alive, there was something awakening in the fish. The more Leah dissolved, the more animated the fish became. There were no longer any barriers between them.

"I have been waiting for you for so long." She could hear herself in its voice as it spoke to her.

Leah fell into her body and felt the fins reawaken. The gone and necessary parts of the fish healed over with the last of Leah's humanity slipping away. She was in the sturgeon and the sturgeon was in her. The unbearableness of living slipped away in the cool water and the heat that been raging in Leah for so long, burned its last ember as it brought the fish back to life.

With the hunters approaching, the sturgeon rolled back into the water. The moon dipped back into the clouds and under the darkness of the sky, the sturgeon escaped the angry mob on the shore of the river. The deeper the fish went, the less sound and noise from above penetrated the joy of being back in the dark and silent water. The sturgeon rode the tides out of the harbor and slipped into the cold and deep waters of the Atlantic Ocean.

Mr. Coop-Dee-Doo of NYC Goes Abroad

On an especially wet and muggy day in September, Coop Chandler found himself in the West Village contemplating a selection of journals in an overcrowded bookstore with no obvious joy in his task. Even the windows were wet with perspiration as more and more people dipped inside to escape to downpour and add to the collective din that roared in Coop's hungover and throbbing head. He had been staring at the notebooks for far too long and already three separate people had reached through Coop's field of vision to grab their selections with obvious vexation. Coop was far too weary to care. That's where his life had led him and dropped him off unceremoniously: weariness, with a touch of perpetual exhaustion.

He sighed and reached for the plainest pocket-sized notebook. He chose that particular one for its efficiency and practicality, with little regard to the style or joy it brought him. After several uncomfortable shuffles and side steps, Coop wriggled his way into the travel section, which was dishearteningly sparse. He shifted through books of sunny escapes with turquoise oceans and bright beaches, before landing on a book on Scotland, of which there was only one. With its history of battles and brawls, a distillery around every corner, more history of drunken adventures and misadventures, and pre-war cars for sale in the front yards of farmhouses, Scotland, he thought, was a country held as testament to the wildness of man, which was exactly what he needed. He was tired of being cooped up Coop.

With his journal and travel book in tow, Coop waited in the short line that seemed to take for too long, feeling itchy and anxious. Eschewing the paper bag, which would only get wet anyway he grumbled, he tucked the journal and book inside his raincoat and jogged around the corner to an old bar called The Stag he had frequented when he was younger. His wife, correction his *ex-wife*, he thought to himself, had hated it and so he never went back out of some kind of misplaced respect for invalidating his tastes for hers, which was, like most things involving that woman, a mistake.

The place smelled just as it had all those years ago, he thought as he sidled up to the bar, breathing in the combination of stale beer and liquor mixed with a cleaning astringent that never seemed to get the stickiness off of the counters. He looked up to the emblem of the stag above the bar, remembering the long and groggy nights he had enjoyed in his younger days. He remembered how the stag would seem to move and shake its head as if it were speaking directly to him. Sometimes he swore it would wink. He chuckled for the first time all day at the thought, remembering that liveliness of those nights "with the boys."

"Scotch," he said to the bartender. "Oban if you got it," he added.

"We got it," the bartender said with a nod to his travel book, "Getting in the mood for your trip?"

"Sure," Coop chuckled, "just trying to get out of the rain and 'in the mood' as you say."

"When are you going?" The bartender asked as he slid the glass over to Coop.

"Tomorrow," said Coop as he took the glass and lifted it to cheers the bartender and the stag.

"Whoa," replied the bartender, "bit late to be planning a trip."

"Well, it wasn't exactly something that was in the cards until recently." The scotch softened his steeliness. "I'm in recovery from matrimony," he said.

"Going stag these days then? Don't blame you."

"Right," Coop said enjoying the pun more than he might have. "I'm getting out the city after a brutal divorce to a woman I don't know why I married in the first place." He finished his drink with a long drag. "Another one, make it a double if you please. I'm particularly thirsty today it seems."

"Thirsty?" The bartender said as he poured the scotch and added a glass of water for good measure. "What exactly do you think you're thirsting for?"

110

Coop was about to reply before the bartender was pulled away by another customer. Just as well, thought Coop, as he ignored the water and drank the scotch. He wasn't sure how he would have replied. He looked up at the stag, feeling more comradery between himself and the carved beast than his fellow human companions. He wondered, what was he thirsting for anyway?

***

Coop drove past a little gathering of buildings: a tea cottage, a sheep farm, and a few homes dotted in between. Limbs of moss-covered trees crouched low to the ground as if the trees might stand up and walk at will. Clumps of stones and heather hugged the ground between the rising roots. The green of the moss broke through the otherwise grey morning. Coop flipped on the windshield wipers as a soft mist dropped from the sky.

The road progressed smoothly around the edge of a lake that had been, until now, hidden from Coop's view. Dark waters lurched idly as rain drops disturbed its surface. Coop found himself fascinated with the darkness of the color. The water seemed to draw in the very greenness of its surroundings until it concentrated into a dark pine hue. A crumbling stone cottage set back from the road clung to the edge of the lake. Smoke billowed from its chimney.

He had the strongest sense of *home* here in Scotland that he could not place. He imagined it must have been some school boy fantasy that he had concocted long ago, but had forgotten. Remembering his pocket-sized notebook, he imagined jotting down: *The vast wilderness here reflects the wildness of the spirit.*

Coop drove through the highlands, making his way past Aberdeen, Inverness, and Loch Ness, and was now in Oban. He chose to come here for reasons that were unknown to him at the time, although he told people it was a love of their scotch and the way he could taste the sea in it. Now, he wondered what kind of life he would have lived never

111

knowing about this small fishing town on the coast of Scotland. To some, it might not seem like much, just a few houses clinging to the hillside along the edge of the dark cold water. To Coop, it was the kind of place he had read about long ago, a place for dark mysteries and adventure.

Despite the chilly autumn air, he rolled down the window to breathe in the damp smell of the sea. The sun had not quite set, but the sky was just dark enough so that the lights of the shops and pubs twinkled brightly. He drove through the roundabout in the center of town and followed the road along the coastline. The grand weathered inns on the edge of the sea glowed warmly against the backdrop of the dark ocean. Coop spotted guests in the dining rooms sitting along the windows as they ate. He loved how Scottish inns and hotels had homely dining rooms.

Coop had done quite a bit of traveling in his day as an M&A broker for corporate banks. Flying from city to city, bank to bank, he would get lost in the big and impersonal hotels that were forever directing guests to the nearest chain restaurant. Not here, he thought. With its warm hearths and cold ale, Scotland was a place that respected the tradition of the weary traveler.

"In 400 hundred feet, please, turn right." The GPS stated as he approached the inn. "Arrived." He pulled into the driveway. The house loomed so high that Coop had to crane his neck to see the top. It looked as if it had been painted red once, but the paint had faded long ago from the unending force of the winds and the salt of the sea. A garden of rose beds and gnomes surrounded the house. Along the path of crushed oyster shells there was a white fence with a gate at the end. He saw a light turn on in the hallway. Coop opened the hatchback of the car, removed his suitcase from the back in one motion, and made his way along the path.

He pushed the door open and looked around the place. It was smaller inside than he had thought, more of a hallway than an atrium. There was standard hotel fare: an end table by the door with a bell, brochures, and local made shortbread for sale. The wallpaper was lilac with a repeating pattern of

Scottish thistles in black. Antiques of varying sizes were strategically placed around the room; copper bells in a glass case, silver candlesticks on the chest of drawers, and old books in dusty shelves. Vintage silhouette portraits hung on the walls. The place was small, dark, and—Coop thought—cozy. He pressed the little bell on the table.

A stout man with a red beard and bushy hair flecked with salt and pepper shading walked into the hallway. "Hello! You must be Mr. Coop."

"Mr. Ch—"

"Your room is all set," interrupted the innkeeper as he opened a cabinet and pulled out a bronze key with an oversized tassel at the end. "Here you go Mr. Coop."

"Mr. Chandler."

"We're all set now, follow me."

"Thanks." Coop picked up his bag and followed the innkeeper up the winding staircase.

"We're a bit empty right now, so I put you at the very top. It's quite a hike, but you have a lovely view of the harbor."

"I'm sure it will be just fine."

As they passed the landings on each floor, Coop noticed again the vintage curios that decorated the end tables and buffets—worn books, pocket watches, thin reading glasses, ceramic plates, and a few old keys here and there—but what was most interesting were the glass bell jars etched with numbers. Coop had seen this trend back home in the city, where decorators would take old fashioned bell jars and put things under them, things like driftwood and sea shells for beach houses, moss and stones for patios, and brass bibelots for studies. Here, the innkeeper had employed the same decorating techniques in a similar fashion, except for what was held underneath the dome glass ceilings. Dried bunches of herbs, antlers, rusted knives, arrowheads, moss covered rocks, and animal skulls filled the bell jars. Coop shuddered as he walked past them.

The two men approached the final landing, which was smaller than the others with only two doors. Instead of the strange baubles Coop had noticed earlier, this landing was lined with shelves that held heavy leather books. By the staircase there were two worn upholstered reading chairs. Between them was a small round table with a reading lamp that provided the only light for the floor.

"Here we are!" The innkeeper said cheerfully as he pushed the bronze key into the lock.

Inside, the windows were large and allowed for a clear view of the small town on the water's edge. Compared to the rest of the house, the room was simple. There was a bed, a chair, and a little stand with a coffee pot and some snacks for sale. Coop set down his bag.

"Not bad," said Coop as he pulled back the thistle patterned curtains.

"Will you be needing dinner reservations this evening?"

Coop moved away from the window. "What's good around here?"

"My brother runs a lovely little seafood place on the water."

"Your brother?" Coop inquired.

"Seven sons in all!" Said the innkeeper as he fluffed the pillows and smoothed the bedspread. "I have a special reserve bottle from the distillery," he said with a grin. "If you'd like to join me for a drink?"

Coop shrugged, "I'll come down in bit." He gave him a nod. "Thank you."

Coop sat on the bed and looked at the two pillows, stuffed and full. He pulled back the cover and let his hand pass over the sterile roughness that comes from too many washings and not enough usage. Coop had felt this fabric too many times before on his business trips. As he felt it now, he felt an anger begin to boil, slow at first, as he rubbed his hand across the fabric. The starched fibers tore at his skin and he grew angrier and angrier with each pass. In a burst of fury, he threw it across the room where the pillow landed with a soft thud. After a while had passed, he got up, opened his suitcase, took out his doc kit, and went to the bathroom.

He wondered just when and where his life had taken such a strange and unnatural turn. His job and his marriage had felt obligatory, as if he were pretending to be something he wasn't, but both of those were over now. There was a joylessness and emptiness that haunted him. Certainly, he hadn't lived the kind of life he had wanted for himself when he was young, when the days seemed impossibly long and life eternally endless, the toy truck in his hand reflecting the sun's last light as he sat in his family's backyard with the smell of summer heavy in the air and the lights of the fireflies blossoming amongst the trees.

As a young boy, he had felt a wildness about him, something that felt raw and untamed, a wild beating that was absent amongst his friends and family. At times he had felt downright savage. He felt as if he fought the urge to run into the woods and rub dirt and leaves against his smooth skin, to claw at the earth and feel the live thing beating inside of it. Sitting there in the fading summer's light, he had heard it, that beating from far off that called out to him. But as he stood on the verge of answering, he heard his mother's voice from the house, calling him to come and wash before dinner. Fighting the two, he had made a choice. He went inside.

The memory shook something loose in his mind. Until now, he had forgotten almost entirely about it. Now, as he looked out into the harbor dotted with roughhewed fishing boats, he wondered if that moment wasn't a key to unlocking the complicated puzzle of choices and outcomes that composed his life. If only he had answered that call of the wild on that day . . . then what? He took out his notebook and wrote: *I want to be the wild thing.*

***

Coop walked down the stairs and glanced at the passing windows. The lights of the boats mesmerized him as they illuminated the dark backdrop of the water. He could seem himself there on a fishing boat, counting the cash from the catches of the day over glasses of scotch with friends.

Instead, he thought bitterly, his days had been spent in an undignified cubicle with a desk drawer full of individually wrapped snacks to help him pass the hours with as little boredom as he could manage. He was glad to be rid of it.

The steps of the staircase wound down to the ground floor where Coop followed the gentle sounds of clinking. In a little nook of a parlor, the innkeeper rifled through an old cabinet pulling out bottles of scotch and replacing them after careful examination. Smells of tobacco and old wood wafted through the room. Two leather-winged back chairs sat in front of a grand mantelpiece, where a fire burned.

"Nice little set up you got here," Coop said as he felt the old leather with his fingertips, imagining the years of cigar smoke and fireside chats.

"A little indulgence I afford myself at the end of the day," the innkeeper replied, bringing out a smudged bottle from the cabinet. He poured generously into two crystal tumblers and signaled for Coop to sit down as he brought over the glasses.

"That's some damn fine drink you got there." Coop said after he executed an expert sip. He sat down slow and let the warmth of the spirit and the comfort of the chair fill his body.

"So. What brings you to Scotland?" The innkeeper gave an approving nod and swirled the liquid around the glass. He set the drink on his knee.

"Drinking," Coop lifted his glass, "lots and lots of drinking."

"That doesn't seem so bad."

"Doesn't it?" Coop swallowed. "That's an odd taste. What is it?"

"They tell me they make it out of the sea water from the bay out there." He nodded towards the harbor, "but I wouldn't believe them if I were you."

"Huh," said Coop as he watched the fire dance and blossom across the garret. Was it him or was there a liveliness to the flames, perhaps a certain redness that hadn't been there before? Their movements soothed him as he sat deeper in his chair.

"I know this might be prying, but I'm wondering why you're traveling all by yourself." The innkeeper rubbed the edges of the glass with his thumb and forefinger.

"You know how these things are," Coop sighed. He had grown tired of talking about it and rehashing when and where he had gone so wrong with his life. Coop twiddled his thumb against the glass and tried to ignore the eyes of his host being drawn towards the pale band around his finger.

"I see." The innkeeper said.

Coop looked at a framed silhouette of a stag above the fire. The animal stood at the edge of a crag; its head lifted high. He couldn't be sure, but he was certain that a spark electrified the painting for a second and faded. Coop shook his head and looked at his drink.

"Something wrong?"

"Nothing." It was only a trick of the flames, Coop told himself. "Better get going then before I miss dinner." He set the glass down on the little end table. "You said the place was on the water?"

"Along the water, just past the fisherman at the end of the wharf." The innkeeper smiled as he gestured with his free hand. "Good night to you!"

"Good night," said Coop with a casual salute.

***

Sitting solo at a table for two, Coop slurped oysters from Loch Lomond with white wine from France. For the main course he dined on a sea bass with creamed leeks and savory mash. All the while he sat and watched the ships coming in and out of the sound. Passengers traveling from Mull and the outer islands arrived back at the little harbor town: tourists carried bags full of trinkets from Iona, bearded men in sturdy pants traveled home with salty looking dogs for companions, and families with little ones held their coats against the wind. All around him happy friends, families, and

117

lovers clattered their silverware as the denizens of the little harbor town made their last entreaties before night fall.

"So," a voice boomed behind Coop, "you're the American."

Coop started at the sight of a tall burly man with dark hair and green eyes. "The other brother?" He asked.

"I see you don't waste time or food." The man took the empty plate from Coop's table.

"I've been here for over an hour."

"Hm," he snorted as he cleared away the crumbs with a quick stroke. "That's what I'm always hearing about you Americans . . . fast food and all. Time is money. That sort of thing."

"That's me," Coop said as he downed the rest of his wine.

"If you're not doing anything afterwards, you should go to my brother's bar across the way."

"Are you guys the Oban mafia or something?"

"What?"

"Never mind. Where's his pub?"

The brother pointed inland. "Just down the way. Can't miss it. Giant image of a stag on the outside. Tell him I sent you."

"And what's your name?"

But the brother was gone. In place of the plate, there was the check for his meal.

***

Evening had past and night fell upon the little Scottish town by the time Coop left the restaurant. He pulled his coat tight around his ears as he stepped into the autumn chill. Most businesses, for pleasure and purpose, had closed long ago. He pulled out his little notebook and made a note: *I've been inside for far too long. Out there, the sea asks: What am I thirsty for?* He replaced his notebook in the back pocket of his khakis. Across the way was a warmly lit pub with an etching of a stag

118

in the window. Coop crossed the street and pulled at the heavy oak door.

Inside the sounds of hearty laughter and glasses hitting the thick wood of the bar filled the air. Coop felt the immediate sense of ease that comes from walking into a bar anywhere in the world and knowing exactly the experience he was going to get. Coop pulled out a stool at the bar and waited. Thick candles illuminated the unusually dark pub. Patrons passed in and out of shadows.

"Ah! And you must be Mr. Coop!" Said the cheery bartender. He placed an empty glass in front of Coop.

"Was there a town announcement about me?" Coop asked.

"Not a town announcement," said the bartender as he poured scotch from a smudged bottle, "but you have caused quite a stir amongst my brothers. He pointed to three of the patrons at the end of the bar: a gruff and stout man with a bushy red beard, a taller gentleman that filled out his form with overbearing muscles, and a pleasant looking fellow with round features and a face that reflected his cheerful demeanor.

"I suppose you've met just about all of us by now." He told me.

"To your health, Mr. Coop," said the man with the red beard as he lifted his glass and nudged his companions to do likewise.

"Cheers," Coop said as he lifted his glass in return and downed the drink. He shook his head vigorously as the fiery liquid poured down his throat. "I don't know how you boys do it, but damn if you don't have the best scotch I've ever tasted."

The three brothers laughed and continued their conversation in lowered voices.

"So," the bartender said as he poured Coop another round. He pushed the glass towards him, "you're here for a little of the old rest and relaxation?"

"You could say that," Coop sipped his second glass. He pointed to his bare ring finger. "Oh hell, I'll just say it. I'm divorced." He downed the glass. "But I'm sure you've heard all that by now."

119

"My brother said you seemed like the kind of man that had been kept inside for too long," the bartender said as he put down the glass.

"You married?" Coop looked up at the bartender.

"Me?" He leaned forward onto the bar with crossed arms. "No—none of my brothers are married, actually. Not the type."

"Maybe guys like us don't sit well next to porcelain china," Coop said as held the glass to the light and rolled the liquid around the edges before bringing it back down to his lips.

"Don't misunderstand me, but I don't see you as a wild man, Mr. Coop."

"I know, I know . . . I've been too tamed." Coop said as he waved his hand. He brought his index and thumb finger inches apart, "I've been pushed into these little spaces." Coop pushed his fingers closer together, "a cubicle," he brought them even closer, "a condo," he said. "I've been pushed and pushed until I couldn't get any smaller," he squashed both fingers together. Coop curled his hand into a fist and lowered it slowly on the bar.

"And now?" The bartender asked.

"Well, I've been thinking about staying here and finding a place on the outer islands. You know? Just living my life and not having to worry about things so much anymore."

"Wouldn't you be missed?"

"Doubt it." He drained his glass. "Hell, I think everyone halfway wishes I wouldn't come back home after the pain in the ass I've been to them. Nah, everyone's sick of me."

"I've heard that once or twice, but with you, I think it's true." The bartender refilled Coop's empty glass. "Since my brothers seem to have taken to you, drinks are on me tonight," he said as he began stacking cleaned glasses, "but since no one here is actually paying, I'll close up and head to the inn so we can drink on *his* tab." He winked at Coop. "I imagine everyone is already there."

"Everyone?" Coop asked.

He looked around to find the bar empty. He peered into his empty glass, wondering just how long he had gone on about everything.

"We're getting together to celebrate your visit to Oban, Mr. Coop!" Said the pleasant looking brother at the end of the bar answered.

"Ignore them," said the bartender. He slapped down his rag and wiped the counter. "You three, put those stools on the bar and make yourself useful."

"Are you sure I can't pay you?" Asked Coop as he dug through his pockets.

"No, in fact," he reached under the bar for the smudged bottle of scotch, "you take this with you." He winked. "Go on then."

"Well, don't mind if I do," Coop stood up and swigged from the bottle.

"That's the spirit, Mr. Coop," the stocky brother from the end of the bar said as he came up and slapped Coop on the back.

"Mr. Coop-dee-doo," Coop said with a crooked smile.

Together the four men walked through the streets that were now silent and dark. Mist rolled in from the sea and mixed with the light from the streetlamps, making the town appear as if it were on fire from an invisible flame that crawled inland with long fingers, grasping at random for its prey. A breeze blew at billows that curled and disappeared into the darkness.

Coop walked next to the brothers as they laughed at rude jokes while punching and wrestling at intermediate intervals. Coop found speech to be increasingly difficult, never mind walking. He staggered and tried to concentrate on cobblestones slipping underneath his feet. Every now and then he took a swig from the bottle.

As the brothers approached the water, they began to whoop. One would start and another would copy, until soon enough all three were downright howling. In the wildness of it, something pulled at Coop from deep within and he let it bubble and pour out of the dungeon he had made for it so long

121

ago. An animalistic urge came over him and he wanted to get on all fours and claw at the earth. He felt it emerge from his throat and he whooped and howled like an animal with the brothers.

When the pack of them were in earshot of the inn, Coop heard the howling and shouting in return. He stumbled over a garden gnome as they crossed the crushed oyster shells past the gate and his stomach churned. About now, he regretted his choice in seafood for the night. They clambered onto the porch and burst through the door into the house.

"Guess we won't be waking anyone up?" asked Coop.

"Lucky for us," said a brother (he couldn't tell which) nudging Coop in the ribs, "you're the only guest."

Coop rubbed his head. "Maybe I should go to bed—"

"Nonsense!" Another brother came and ushered Coop into the room, "Come join us!"

Sounds of hearty laughter and shouting erupted from the room. Inside, seven chairs sat in a semi-circle around a roaring fire. The smells of sweat and alcohol pierced the otherwise homeliness of the space. Above the intricately carved grand fireplace hung a large stag's head with a magnificent pair of horns that almost touched the ceiling. The chairs were a mismatch of wing-backed leather chairs, solid wooden table chairs, and patterned reading chairs. Coop recognized most of the brothers, except for one with long red hair down his back and a long red beard to match. He must be the one who works at the distillery, thought Coop. Sensing his stare, the man turned to look at him.

"To you!" He said as he lifted his glass.

Coop smiled and returned the favor with a swig from the bottle. Lucky too, Coop thought, its contents were almost gone. He settled into a particularly comfortable looking chair.

"And how was your evening?" The innkeeper asked.

"Ex-ce-lent," Coop replied with a cockeyed smile.

The seven brothers sat and passed around drinks, pipes, and cigars. Smoke billowed up towards the ceiling. Coop felt an intoxicated stupor begin to grow in his body. He slumped in his seat and gave into warmth of the room.

"What's with the head?" Coop muttered as he pointed to the stag.

"The family crest is a stag," replied the bartender.

"That's what we say in public."

"Don't go messing with him again."

"Go on, tell him the story."

"What story?" Coop's head bounced from one brother to the next, barely able to keep up with who was who, never mind who said what. In his haze, the brothers' bodies melted into an amalgam of hair and muscle.

The brother with the long red hair stood up and rested his arm on the fireplace. "You want to hear it?"

"Now, now, he doesn't need all that gibberish," said the innkeeper.

"No, I do," said Coop as he sat up a little taller. "Tell me."

"Long, long ago," the brother with the long red hair began, "there were seven brothers that lived in the Highlands. One day, they all went out hunting in the outer isles to the north." He crouched low as if hunting in the forest. "The brothers followed the tracks of a stag deep into the woods, but these weren't any ordinary stag tracks, no, no. These were the largest tracks they had ever seen. What the brothers didn't know was that this wasn't an ordinary creature, but an old Druid priest that had given himself eternal life through the body of the stag."

Coop felt his eyelids droop as his shoulders slumped. The heat of the room was rising in direct proportion to Coop's drowsiness.

"So," the brother smiled, "when the most handsome and daring red headed brother," he ducked the little objects his brothers threw at him, "had the stag in his sight." He crouched and made a motion of drawing back an arrow, "the brother took his shot and pierced the stag in the heart!"

The brothers' mock gasps of shock awoke Coop from his drowsiness. He lifted his head and tried to keep his eyes open but had little luck. His night was through and he was

123

ready for bed, but before he could excuse himself the brother went on again.

"They followed the trail of blood dripping through the trees and found the creature on the forest floor in a clearing. As they approached, it lifted its head and spoke, telling them that he was an enchanted creature and would return to the forest again. But," he lifted his finger, "the brothers would be cursed to live forever alone with each other until they could return the stag to his home in the forest."

"But how would they know? Coop roused his head. "Sorry?"

"How would the brothers know it was the stag?"

"Some say the stag will come to them," suggested one brother.

"Others say the brothers take a man and turn him."

"And the brothers?" Asked Coop.

"To this day, there are those that say the brothers still live in the highlands, waiting and waiting for the stag to come home."

"Enough of that!"

Once the spell of the story had been spun, the brothers returned to their carousing. The quiet of the room once again erupted into a din of laughter and bawdy jokes. Coop tried to excuse himself but found that he didn't have the strength or will to leave the warmth of the room. He dropped his head to his chin and let the bottle slip from his grasp to the floor. Someone picked it up and put it back in the crook of his arm. Coop rolled to the other side of the chair and curled into his legs and arms.

He felt someone strong lift him. Coop tried again to move but found his body too heavy and his mind too muddled. Instead, he let himself drift deeper into an inevitable sleep. He felt the chill of the air outside and smelled the salt of the sea. Sounds of feet marching beat in his ears. What a strange dream he was having, thought Coop. Someone placed his body in a rough bed of nets and ropes. Men's voices bubbled around him, but he couldn't understand their words. Someone whispered in his ear and he gave a little nod. There was a bump and a splash as he felt himself being pushed forward into the water. There he drifted as the waves lapped against the sides of a boat and he felt himself drift into a deep slumber.

***

The moonlight poked through Coop's sleeping eyes and jolted him awake. The boat rocked with the rhythm of the waves as they slapped against its sides. Stars shone down through an open sky. Underneath the ghostly light, Coop stirred amongst the tangle of tackles and fishing lines around him. He tightened his grip when he saw he was adrift. How had he gotten here? It seemed as if no time had passed between now and when he had fallen asleep in the parlor.

Instead of the pain or lethargy he expected to feel from his overindulgence, he felt energized as a pulse beat from somewhere within him. The evening's events were blurred in Coop's mind, as if he knew the answers but had forgotten them entirely. Coop clutched at his head as his thoughts battled one another for the slippery grip of his reality.

Just ahead of the boat, Coop caught sight of a pebbled beach with dark rocks. He found an oar beneath his feet and with a few ungainly attempts at paddling, the boat at last moored on the shallow bottom. Trees cast shadows upon the rocky coast. The moon's light revealed the small beach. Darkness lingered in the thick forest beyond the shore. Coop's head turned at a movement in the trees, only to realize it must have been a trick of the light, for nothing and no one, stirred.

As he stepped out of the boat, his shoes slipped against the smooth rocks and he was cast into the cold sea water. Salt stung against his tongue. Goose bumps bubbled up through his skin. His body shook and sweat covered his skin. He felt as if a snake of teeth and fire exploded from within and he found himself throwing up into the water. Instead of the contents of dinner, he watched as his memories flowed out of his mouth. Sound and color moved within the images as they floated away in the current. His chest moved in short and shallow

125

spurts and his body shivered. With the last of his energy, Coop crawled towards the land.

He laid upon the shore like that for a while. He was nowhere in his mind; not really there or here either. There was a deep unshaking belief that something had been wiped clean. A mistake had been unmade. If he had a feeling that his life was not his, then it existed no longer. Coop was never supposed to be the husband to his ex-wife or the son of his mother. He had been just an extra soul clogging the machine.

The stag was never meant to die. The brother's story rang through the emptiness of his mind and Coop realized he had been set back upon the earth in hopes of making it right. For every lifetime, a piece of the puzzle was set back into motion. Each action set into motion an outcome, all with the goal of having begun and ended something. Finally, Coop understood. The brothers had set him free.

A soft stirring of voices rang clear through the silence. Coop stirred at the suddenness of the sound. His skin prickled as he sensed something much older than the whole of humanity surround him. Sounds of voices singing and whispering bounced through the air. Coop turned his head as the voices returned towards the forest and paused, waiting for him to join them. Surefooted now, he lifted himself off the ground to follow them. Sand turned to pebbles. Small stones turned to rocks. Coop climbed up and over the last of the rock face. At the rock's edge, he removed his shoes. He padded upon the soft forest floor, certain of his step. A deep sense of trust pulled him deeper into the woods. Coop had heard the call.

He walked past a rowan tree, and another, and another. His clothes felt tight and hot upon his skin. Coop pulled off his shirt and left it on a branch. On another he hung his pants. One by one he removed each piece of clothing and laid them on the branches like offerings. The cool evening breeze wrapped itself around him. Coop felt wild and free.

Soft lights formed from the darkness and floated in the knotted branches. Like fireflies, they would light up a tree here or a bush there. Coop felt reassured by their presence, as

126

if the offering of clothes had been accepted by the spirits. He felt a part of them, as they moved like a procession deeper and deeper into the woods. Letting the wildness within him break forth, Coop hooted and howled with all his might into the air.

Wild whoops and yells reverberated through the trees in response. A clearing appeared through the trees. In its center rested a marble alter with the head of a stag with a magnificent pair of horns. Around the alter stood large grey stones with curled markings weaving into the rock face.

A loud crash like thunder burst through the trees and the stones transformed into men. Their flesh, muscles, and thick hair erupted from the rocks. They jumped with their furs and feathers, whooping, dancing and calling to one another. The air filled with the pounding of their feet on the earth. Behind the alter stood a tall figure with red hair so long and thick it covered its face and dropped low to the ground.

Coop moved into the clearing and past the dancing brothers. They nudged him with their spears and the tips of their bows. Some clapped him on the back as he past them. The brothers beat their hands in rhythms upon the earth.

He moved towards the alter and approached the man behind it. With a soft nod of recognition, he opened his arms to his sides. The brother lifted the stag's head and placed it over Coop. Lights and voices lit the air like fire and shined through the dark. A beating from the earth pulsed. The figures hushed and stopped.

Soft skin bristled and burned as a grey coat covered Coop's body. Fingers and toes lengthened into hooves as his legs grew longer and fuller. His ribs rounded and ballooned until they held a giant cavity of organs. His body lengthened and expanded. A soft tail emerged from his rump. The animal shook and a soft spray of silver flickered in the lights. The animal lifted its head. At last, the stag had come home.

Vintners

Enzo picked at the dirt in his nails while he waited for the others. This year's harvest was already looking promising, but it would be the grapes from last year's harvest they would be drinking tonight. He sat at the old wooden table and unconsciously tapped a steady beat with his foot, which he was only vaguely aware of by the soft knocking sounds it made in the quiet evening.

Crumbling head stones and mausoleums dotted the soft and wet ground where the grapes grew in unsteady lines. Enzo set his focus upon on a small tree that had been planted long before the grapes were ever there. He sat and thought at how a tree could die a hundred times in the frost of winter before its life was done. A voice called out from behind him.

"Lend a hand to these old bones!"

"Late and begging, Luc?" Enzo replied. Despite his words, he rose to take the full jugs of wine and placed them on the table with two heavy thuds.

Enzo heard the soft beat of the bells first, and then the clear voice rolling over the hill singing an unknown song. He waited for her silhouette to come rising up the steep incline, unaware that he was tapping his fingernail against the glass of the wine bottle in tune with the jingle of her bells.

"Together again," the singer said as she placed her basket on the table. With a swish of her skirt, she sat herself down amongst the others.

"You always bring too much, Ro" Enzo grumbled.

"Ritual has its place," Ro said as she laid out the loaves of bread and fresh picked fruit.

"Eh, that's why you get all the serious ones, Enzo," tsk'd Luc as he pulled his hat off and wiped his brow.

"You've always had a penchant for the more litigious ones," Ro said as she poured out the wine.

"Lawyers, doctors, accountants, generals . . ." Luc listed, "they all find you. Me? I get the travelers and the sea folk."

"I do love a good artist," Ro nodded in agreement. "But of course, we don't pick the dead, the dead pick us." She raised her glass and the others followed.

"To the dead!" Luc said.

"To the stories they tell us," Enzo muttered as he lifted his glass with the others.

He drank the wine like a necessary tonic, but no longer enjoyed it the way he once did. Each drink filled his whole body with thoughts, emotions, and experiences drawn out of the bodies below the earth. He had lived a thousand lives by now. As Enzo let the bitter liquid run down his throat, the stories burned in his body. He knew he could never say no to the dead that so desperately wanted to be heard. Where he had once been alive, he now felt as if the dead were the ones living and he were the one deteriorating beneath the earth.

S.N. Kirby received a B.A. in English with a concentration in creative writing from Tulane University in New Orleans, and graduated from The New School's MFA program in Creative Writing. Her creative work centers on the nexus of man, magic, and nature. With roots in magical realism and fables, her stories infuse magic and mystical transformation into character focused storytelling. *Lunatiques* is the author's debut work.

The author lives in New York City with her two big dogs and husband.